Once There Were Green Fields

Once There Were Green Fields

Paul: God bless you :)

RANDY PEASE

Randy Pease
02/16/15

authorHOUSE®

AuthorHouse™ LLC
1663 Liberty Drive
Bloomington, IN 47403
www.authorhouse.com
Phone: 1-800-839-8640

Published by AuthorHouse 08/07/2014

ISBN: 978-1-4969-2952-5 (sc)
ISBN: 978-1-4969-2984-6 (e)

CONTENTS

Foreword vii

Prologue xi

    April 5, 1968 xi

Rewind: Pre-Season 1

    August 15, 1961 1
    The Chute 3
    The Fieldhouse 9
    Parkway 12
    The Hustler 15
    Labor Day 18
    First Day of School 20

The Season 23

    First Game 23
    A Thunder of Drums 30
    Repentance 32
    Central 34
    Flyboy 46
    The Edict 47
    Home 49
    Fall Festival 52
    Home Again 56
    Hit the Road, Jack 57

Exile..62

Gas Station..64

Homecoming 67

The Dance 71

Busted 74

The Deluge 77

Bullshit to Baloney 79

Undefeated, Untied, Unscored Upon.....................83

Post-Season 86

Orbits and Obits 86

Graduation...89

Diaspora...92

We've Got to Get Out of this Place 93

Bus Station...95

July 1972 97

Benny...99

Forty Years Later… 101

November 2011 104

Jill 112

Martha... 116

Where the Boys Are 121

The Dream 124

Recovery 125

Comic Relief...127

In Search of Ricky Ferrell....................................128

Epilogue...133

About the Author...135

FOREWORD

"The story ends, yeah; it was no lie. Names have
been changed, dear, to protect you and I."
The Jive Five - 1961

Back in the 1960s, Kurt Vonnegut set out to write a factual account of the Dresden bombings during World War II. The story, unknown to most Americans, needed to be told, and Vonnegut, who had survived the bombing, reasoned that he was the guy best equipped to do it. After interviewing as many survivors as he could find, he hurriedly hammered out his first draft, which turned out to be neither very long nor very interesting. In the interest of better storytelling, he kept working on it, enhancing and embellishing it, adding to it and subtracting from it. The end result, *Slaughterhouse Five*, is barely tethered to the truth at all.

Such were the problems I encountered in the early drafts of this manuscript.

My original plan was to chronicle the 1961 season of the Reitz Panthers, an extraordinary high school football team that rolled through its entire season without allowing a point. (The feat had never been accomplished before, and it has not been accomplished since.) I also wanted to put a magnifying glass on the autumn of 1961 to see how events that unfolded locally, nationally, and globally during that year have affected who we are now. A third goal was to follow up on the '61 Panthers to see what direction their lives have taken since that unblemished season.

Originally, I wanted to record that season in a straight journalistic fashion, using interview material and archival news clippings as my source material, but the more I wrote, and the more anecdotes I collected, the more I came to realize that journalism might not be the best vehicle to tell this story. As I typed these anecdotes, they begged to be written as scenes or chapters that, when stitched together, would form a much broader, richer narrative.

Having already written and read more than one hundred pages, I made a bold decision: to abandon my original scheme and take on a new rhetorical tack, one which, if handled with care and sensitivity, would bring the characters and their story more to life.

With that idea in mind, I wrote and read almost one-hundred more pages before I came to another powerful realization: I was wandering pretty far from the truth. I found myself making up dialogue – writing what people might have said instead of what they actually said. More than forty years have passed, I rationalized. No one really knows what was said – not exactly anyway -- and just about all the people I spoke to had slightly different recollections. I found myself making up things that might have occurred in the interest of perking up the narrative, rationalizing all the while that "might" somehow makes right.

The characters are great: two all-state tackles, one an honor student and eagle scout, the other a ne'er do well from the wrong side of the tracks, both of whom would die in Vietnam; a fullback who played eleven years in the NFL; identical twins at left and right end; a running back whose problems with the law continued until his adult years; a player who quit the team his senior year who became a helicopter pilot in Vietnam and would pick up his dead teammate on a battlefield in the Quang Tri Province in 1968; a coach revered by some, reviled by others...

The 1961 Reitz Panthers really did go through an entire football season without yielding a point, and they really were proclaimed the mythical Indiana state football champions that year. Perhaps "mythical" is the key word here. What I want to do is to enhance the mythology of the 1961 Panthers and pay tribute to their extraordinary achievements before their memories dim and fade from history altogether.

By the time Kurt Vonnegut finished his final draft of Slaughterhouse Five, he was sick of the whole endeavor and ready to move on. Ditto here. Everything you read here is true – except for those numerous parts I made up.

Prologue

April 5, 1968

The tall grass flattens as my C-46 chopper hovers like a giant dragonfly above the landing zone where exhausted Marines haul their dead and wounded over their shoulders in much the same way my old football coach used to make us carry tackling dummies. More often than I care to think about, I've dropped troops off at the battle zone, only to pick up their bagged bodies a few days later. Often the bodies are disemboweled or dismembered or burned beyond recognition. Crispy critters, we called them.

I ease down into the LZ, a clearing in the jungle about the same size as our old practice field. Barely an hour before, I stood out on the perimeter of the base at An Hoa, smoking some kick-ass weed, staring out toward a line of trees at the edge of a long, grassy field, wondering whether some sharpshooter had me in the cross hairs in the scope of his AK-47, and wishing I was back on the loading dock in Indiana, waiting for my shift to end. That's when Lt.

Mendoza gave me the orders to pick up some KIAs about twenty-five clicks up the road in Quang Tri.

Bursts of gunfire erupt from the palm thicket at the perimeter of the field. I fire back. I puff on a cigarette while the Marines load the day's dead and wounded into the belly of my chopper. Once the belly is full, I lift off amid a hailstorm of bullets, and fueled by adrenaline and THC, skim over the treetops toward the nearest MASH unit. Nobody in his right mind would do this. But for me it is just another day in Hell.

At the MASH I help the medics unload the bodies. On the toe of one of the bodies, all lying side by side on a table, dangles a dog tag that says PFC Ray Moon. I grew up on the west side of Evansville, Indiana, with a kid named Ray Moon. We got in trouble together. We played football on a state championship team – the only high school football team in Indiana history to go through a season undefeated, untied, and unscored upon. He was a hell of a tackle and hell of a teammate. After high school and before Vietnam, we worked together on the Mead Johnson loading dock, loading trucks with Metrecal for overweight baby boomers and Enfamil for the babies they boomed.

I peel back the canvas blanket, and there he is. He is easy to recognize, even with one-third of his skull blown away. The dead soldier's short, squat body is unmistakably

Ray's. I roll up his sleeve. The name "Jill" tattooed on his bicep confirms it. Suddenly the war, which has always seemed distant and surreal even when I am smack-dab in the middle of it, rips into my gut like a piece of shrapnel. What are the odds of picking up the body of your best boyhood friend on a battlefield 13,000 miles from home?

Ray never heard the shot that killed him. No one ever does. The burst of gunfire might have come from a hidden machine gun nest dug into a hillside bunker or from a stand of palm trees. And it happens exactly one day after a sniper's bullet takes the life of Martin Luther King while he stands on a motel balcony in Memphis, looking out over a Promised Land he will not enter. Hell of a deal.

REWIND: PRE-SEASON

AUGUST 15, 1961

The mid-day August sun beats down mercilessly as the 7 a.m. whistle blows at the Mead Johnson plant at the foot of the hill. The temperature is already in the 90s.

"Everybody take a knee!" barks Coach Earl Doggett.

A gray-haired man in his mid-fifties with a slight paunch and a haircut as flat as the clipboard he carries, Coach Doggett is both revered and reviled by his players. We all fear his clipboard, which he would use to coldcock us if we blew a blocking assignment, missed a tackle, or were late boarding the team bus. Ray Moon and I sit on a pile of dummies and stomp sweat bees with our cleats.

"Listen up!" Coach hollers.

I have heard his first day of practice motivational speech three times since my sophomore year, but most of the players stop doing whatever and listen as if they were hearing the Sermon on the Mount: *"Boys, you're all green and unseasoned, blah, blah, blah, and all positions are going to be up for grabs, blah, blah, blah…cuss word, cuss word, blah, blah, blah…"*

1

Blessed are they who sacrifice individual glory for the good of the team, for they shall earn favor with the coaching staff.

Blessed are they who follow orders without question, for they shall see playing time.

Blessed are those who block.

Blessed are those who do not smoke or chase girls. Even though his eyes hide behind green-tinted sunglasses, I know he looks straight at Ricky Ferrell. The Old Man's jowls, white-whiskered like an old dog, move up and down as he rants and chomps on an antacid tablet.

Blessed are those who run every play exactly as it is designed in the playbook and woe unto those who do otherwise.

Blessed are the strong and the fast, for they shall run roughshod over the weak and the slow.

Cursed are they who violate these commandments, for they shall know hell.

Of course I paraphrase. He never says anything like that. Coach sprinkles in a lot more god-damns than Jesus ever thought about using, and in his blind obsession with victory, he favors Captain Ahab more than Jesus. All that is missing is the peg leg. Those who play for him are equally divided into two camps: those who hate his guts and those who worship the ground he walks upon. I belong in the former camp. I hope that

God is nothing like Earl Doggett, who never rewards anyone for doing something good but makes everyone endure hell if they screw up. Even if his methods are questionable, you can't argue with coach's record: five state championships, twelve conference championships, sixteen city championships.

Then the foaming starts. The stress of coaching for thirty years brought on a peptic ulcer, which forces him to pop antacids like M & Ms. They cause the area around his mouth to turn white, and he honest to God looks like he is foaming at the mouth. (Ray always called his halftime oratories peptic talks.) He rants on for several minutes about pride, dedication, and sacrifice and then closes with the motto everyone has heard a hundred times: "A winner never quits, and a quitter never wins." Platitude or beatitude, it is the doctrine that Earl Doggett preaches and his players practice.

THE CHUTE

"Hey, Reavis. Your leg is bleeding," says Ray in the huddle. Sure enough, a rivulet of blood trickles from a mosquito bite, which burst open on the previous play. Tony Reavis dips his index finger into the blood and writes his initials on his calf.

"What the hell does that stand for?" says Ray.

3

"Teddy Roosevelt," says Hog Johnson, our starting center.

"Yeah, I speak softly and carry a big stick," Tony quips.

"That's not what I heard," says Ray.

"Hush up you turds!" barks quarterback Charlie Cassidy. "Spin 22 on seven. Let's go!"

Spin 22 is a simple off-tackle play I have run a million times since my freshman year. We clap, bolt from the huddle, and line up in our single wing formation, which is outdated, even for 1961, but that's the only offense Coach Doggett knows. The scheme dates back to Pop Warner days when footballs were made of pigskin, and everyone wore leather helmets with no faceguards. Thankfully, our scuffed silver helmets have one bar across the chin.

Charlie, Donnie McDowell, and I crouch a few yards behind center, all with hands outstretched. Charlie, in my opinion, is the best quarterback in town, even though most of the sportswriters give that nod to Rex Mundi's Bob Griese. Donnie, a first-team all-state linebacker and fullback, stands 6-3 and weighs 200 pounds, but he seems bigger.

Doug and Tony line up at left and right tackle, respectively. Both earned all-state honors as juniors, and along with Donnie, are the only returning lettermen back from a team that went undefeated and won the state championship the year before – but that is about all they have in common. At 6-4, Tony looks more like a basketball player than a football player. Ray is short and stocky, maybe 5-9 and 210 pounds. Reavis is an honor student and an Eagle Scout. Ray is neither. Tony lives with his parents and two sisters in a suburban home his dad built on the west fringe of Evansville using wood salvaged from the old shipyard where his mom helped build LSTs back during the war. Ray lives with his divorced mother and seven brothers and sisters in a tiny shotgun shack on the west bank of Pigeon Creek in a neighborhood full of interchangeable shotgun shacks, all with steeply pitched roofs and barely enough room to walk between them. Tony is college bound. Ray is destined for a factory or a warehouse. The only trait they share is a passion for smashing the living shit out of whatever unlucky son-of-a-bitch lines up across from them.

Before us lies the practice field, a dusty crater littered with rocks, punched into the side of Reitz Hill, as if a meteor struck there, leaving just enough room to scrimmage. Playing football on the practice field is like playing football on the moon, or at least that's what I imagine it would be like. On the snap count, Hog centers the ball to Charlie, who spins and hands off to me. I shoot toward tackle, where a hole is supposed to magically open at just the right moment, like the timely parting of the Red Sea.

5

Except there is no hole, so I veer to the right, find a crack of daylight, sprint down the sidelines, pick up a block by Kenny Cain, who takes out his twin brother Benny with a vicious block at the knees. Some would call it a dirty play, but that's how we were taught to do it. The Old Man, who coaches wrestling in the winter, preaches that, by using leverage, a small man can take down a much bigger man. The fact that the technique might cause permanent ligament damage to an opponent's knees is of no consequence.

I cut back to the inside, break a tackle, and coast into the end zone, where Ricky Ferrell knocks me down and stomps on my hand with his cleats. It isn't an accident. It is Ricky's way of telling me that I had better not do it again. It doesn't matter that I am his teammate and we have known one another since elementary school. He and I are competing for the starting tailback spot.

"Nice run, Gator," he says, helping me to my feet. "Don't even think about doing it again."

His breath smells of vodka. Whereas most of my teammates drink a little beer on weekends, Ricky sometimes chugs vodka before practice. He's back on the team after missing what would have been his junior year because he was doing time in the Indiana School for Boys for robbing a liquor store. Or maybe it was a gas station. It depends who you talk to. Ricky refuses to talk about it.

He's a mean guy and he looks the part, probably because of his permanent Robert Mitchum squint. While most of the guys on team wear the popular Roger Maris flat-top, Ricky and his cousin Ray Moon wear their hair long. He weighs barely 140 pounds, but he is tough and strong after a year of lifting weights at boys' school.

Once on my feet, I don't think about spiking the football or doing a celebratory dance. Coach wants us to act like we have been in the end zone before. When I toss Coach the football, I expect no congratulations because the Old Man never praises anyone, never mumbles so much as "nice catch" or "nice block." Praise goes to our heads, he believes, and that detracts from his team concept. Even so, I do not expect the ass-chewing that follows.

"Gates!"

"Yes, sir?"

"You run through the god-damned hole you're supposed to run through. Is that clear?"

"But it wasn't open and I...."

"And you thought you'd just freelance, right?"

"Sir, I just...."

"Keep your mouth shut, Gates. Now go run the chute."

Ray snickers.

"You run it too, Moon!" Coach bellows. "Take a tackling dummy with you."

Ray and I shoulder a pair of heavy sweat-soaked tackling dummies and slog toward the chute, a steep, well-worn path up the side of the crater, rimmed by Summit Drive. Over the decades, everyone who played for Earl Doggett had to run the chute. Ray probably had to run it more than anybody.

"The bastard hates me," I huff once out of earshot of the Old Man.

"Don't take it personally," Ray says. "He hates all of us. At least he knows your name. Not everybody can say that – even the seniors. He still can't tell the twins apart until they line up."

Breathing heavily, we trudge up the side of the crater, touch the flagpole, and begin our descent back to the playing field. Once back to the huddle, Coach bellows "Run it again, girls!!!"

So we do. This time, on the way back, Ray wheezes, "Don't look like you're tired when we get back or we'll have to do it again."

We stifle our huffing and puffing, trying not to show any pain, which in the Old Man's eyes, is a sign of weakness.

"You guys don't look tired enough!!" Coach Doggett screams. "Do it again!!!!"

"I hate him," I mutter.

"We all do," says Ray. "We hate him. He hates us. Mutual hate. That's how his system works."

8

"Go get some water!" Coach says once we finish our third trip up the chute and back. "But don't drink it. Swish it around and spit it out."

Even in the August heat, we are forbidden to swallow the water from the field house drinking fountain. I rinse out my palate and spit the water back into the fountain like at the dentist's office. Ray spews on me and laughs.

Unlike the practice field, the game field in Reitz Bowl is well-manicured and watered. Sprinklers gush full-blast to ensure that the grass is lush and green for the season opener against Muncie Central. Reitz Bowl is almost as old as Coach Doggett. Back in the 1920s when workmen were building a retaining wall to keep the school from sliding down Reitz Hill, someone had the bright idea of building a football stadium with concrete bleachers.

"Look at those sprinklers," Ray says. "We should be so lucky."

THE FIELDHOUSE

Ray stands at the lavatory beside me, combing his hair. No matter how much Brylcreme he uses, one rogue forelock always falls across his forehead.

"Hey Ray, are you trying to look like Elvis?" I say.

"I was thinking Superman," says Ray.

"I was thinking Fred Flintstone," Kenny Cain jokes, snapping a rolled up towel inches away from his twin brother's bare ass. I still have trouble telling the twins apart even though I have known them since our days at Centennial Elementary. At 5-10 and 160 pounds, they look alike, dress alike, and comb their hair alike, and their grade point averages are identical down to the third decimal. They are fast too. Benny is maybe a tenth of a second faster over a quarter mile.

"Yabba dabba doo!" Ray howls. "A little dab'll do ya."

"I'll bet Jill loves to get her fingers in your hair, doesn't she?" Kenny says.

"That, my small-peckered friend, is none of your business."

"Hey, Roger Maris hit two home runs today against the White Sox. That's 47 and 48. Do you think Maris or Mantle can catch Babe Ruth?" I ask.

"I don't give a rat's ass. Baseball is a pussy sport. Now if you guys will excuse me, Jill is waiting."

We all know what he means. Jill Henderson is no doubt sitting in her old man's big blue Imperial, as is her custom almost every afternoon, listening to the radio, waiting for Ray to finish practice. Sometimes she has to wait for Ray to finish running the chute, long after everyone else is already in the locker room. After practice they often drive down to Parkway for a burger and a malt and maybe a game of pool. Jill's dad is a cop, and he keeps track of the mileage on his car. If Jill and Ray would go someplace besides Parkway, Officer Henderson would know, and he would confiscate the car keys.

"Where the boys are, someone waits for me," Kenny croons, doing his best Connie Francis.

Hog snaps me in my bare ass with a rolled-up towel and then scampers off somewhere amid the labyrinth of lockers in the field house – an ancient brick building with thin walls, concrete floors, and leaky plumbing.

"I'll get your white ass, you miserable chicken shit!" I holler.

I retrieve a greasy towel from the hamper, roll it in a pool of dirty water, wad it up, crouch behind a bank of lockers, and wait. When the footsteps get close, I leap out and fling the wringing wet towel smack into the face of Coach Doggett, who turns three shades of red before he composes himself. He hoists me up like a forklift, pins my shoulders against the cool, red brick wall and stares me down with watery blue eyes. The veins in his nose turn purple, and his breath smells of tobacco and beer.

"Gates," he hisses in a soft Clint Eastwood voice. His whitish lips barely move, and his whiskered jowls tighten. His words escape through tightly clenched, tobacco-stained teeth, like steam escaping from a pressure cooker.

"Yes, sir?" I whimper.

"Don't ever do that again. Understood?"

"Yes, sir."

"And you will not start in our season opener. Understood?"

He lowers me into a puddle of my own piss and stalks away to the Hilltop Inn to like he does almost every afternoon after practice.

PARKWAY

Jill Henderson wheels her dad's big Imperial into the Parkway parking lot and pulls into a slip alongside the dark green '58 Chevy shared by the Cain twins. The Volkswagen Beetle that belongs to Tony Reavis' old man is parked a few slips down. How Tony and his girlfriend manage to make out in that car is beyond me. But they manage. Also parked there is Ricky Ferrell's black 1950 Chevy, the getaway car in his infamous liquor store heist. When he isn't washing or waxing his car, Ricky can usually be found under the hood or under the chassis performing some kind of automotive maintenance.

I sit in the back seat while Ray and Jill sit in front. Although I live close enough to school to walk home, I don't refuse when they offer me a ride to Parkway. Ray doesn't have a car, and neither do I, but on weekends my dad sometimes lets me borrow the family car, a '58 Buick with automatic transmission.

Jill rolls down the window, and orders two cheeseburgers, a chocolate malt, a large Dr. Pepper, an order of fries, and an order of onion rings. I order a grilled cheese, fries, and a Coke.

"That'll be $10.75," crackles a voice over the intercom. I flip through the rolodex jukebox file and settle on "Bristol Stomp" by the Dovells, "Runaway" by Del Shannon, and "Hit the Road, Jack," by Ray Charles.

"Play 'Big, Bad John'" Ray says.

"Why do you like that lame-ass song anyway?" I ask.

"Have you ever listened to the words?"

"Not really. If it doesn't have a beat, I'm not interested."

"It's about this miner who holds up the timbers in the mine so all the other miners can escape a mine disaster."

"So?"

"So? That's what I do for ungrateful little pricks like you. I open up holes and hold them open long enough for you little guys to run through. I do the dirty work. You get the glory and the headlines."

"Ray, holding is fifteen yards."

"Only if you get caught."

While we wait for our food, a procession of cars, many with tall angular tailfins, circles the parking lot. Within minutes, Martha Mattingly, wearing a pink pinstriped apron and roller skates, delivers our food on a tray and clamps it on the window.

"Look at those fins. They're like sharks," says Martha, shaking her head. "Always prowling. They'll probably die if they stop moving."

As I munch my burger and slurp my soft drink, Jill pops a serious question: "Ray, have you given any thought about what you want to do after high school?"

"Yeah, I've thought about it," Ray mumbles, once he has gulped down his mouthful of cheeseburger.

"What do you want to do?"

"Maybe be a cop like your old man. Or maybe join the Army like mine. Or work on the loading dock at Mead's like Gator's…"

"How about college? You got that football scholarship offer from Louisville a few weeks back. Have you thought any more about that?"

"Yeah but the fine print says you've got to be in the top third of your graduating class. I'm not even in the top two thirds. Besides I hate school. Once I graduate, I don't ever want to go to school ever again. Why are you so concerned about the future all of a sudden?"

"If we're going to get married, I need to know something about what kind of life we're going to have together."

"It'll be fine. I'll take care of you."

"Ray, you can't afford onion rings, let alone a wedding ring. If you could do anything, what would it be, Ray?"

"I'd really like to join the fire department. I always thought being a firefighter would be cool."

"I think that's a good idea."

When they start smooching in the front seat, I excuse myself. I think they have forgotten I am in the car.

THE HUSTLER

Jimmy Dean drawls "Big, Bad John" on the jukebox as Ricky Ferrell leans forward and takes careful aim like a sniper, and blasts the cue ball into the middle of the rack, sending balls scattering in all directions. The one ball rolls in, and he walks the perimeter of the table to assess his next shot. He sucks from his cigarette and lays it on the edge of the table so that the burning end hangs just over the table's edge. I lean against a planter full of plastic plants and chalk my stick.

"Every mornning at the mine, you could see him arrive.
He stood 6 foot 6, weighed 245.

Kind of broad at the shoulders, narrow at the hip
And everybody knew you didn't give no lip to Big John...

"Three ball, corner," Ricky calls.

An inch-long ash from Ricky's cigarette breaks off and plummets to the black and white tile floor. Ricky rattles in the three ball, picks up his cigarette, and paces to the other side of the table.

"Six ball, side," he says, motioning with his stick. He sinks the six, takes aim at the four, and with a powerful stroke, blasts the purple ball into the corner pocket. The cue stops in its tracks, leaving a clear shot at the two.

"Hey Ricky, are you gonna let me have a shot?" I ask.

"Not if I can help it."

He lights another Marlboro red from the pack rolled up his t-shirt sleeve, and offers me a cigarette, which I accept. I inhale too deeply and cough non-stop for thirty seconds. I hold my cigarette between my thumb and forefinger like a Gestapo interrogator.

"First one?" Ricky asks, squinting.

"No," I lie.

"You'll get the hang of it."

Ricky smiles, chalks his stick, and knocks home the two. After sinking the five, six, and seven balls in quick succession, he paces around the green rectangle, which is bathed in a cone of smoky light, and studies his best shot at the eight ball, which is partially eclipsed by the fifteen.

"Will you hurry up and shoot, Ricky?" I complain. "What are you doing anyway?"

"I'm studying the geometry of the table, plotting the angles."

"What the hell do you know about geometry? You've never even had algebra."

"Yes I have. Just never passed it."

"Off the rail, corner pocket," says Ricky, exhaling a cloud of smoke through his nostrils and pointing with the blue tip of his stick.

"You'll never make that shot."

"Five bucks says I will."

"Five bucks is all I've got on me," I protest. "If I lose, I'm flat broke."

"But if you win, you'll have ten dollars. You could take somebody to dinner and a movie – maybe see *The Hustler*. I saw it at the drive-in last week. That Paul Newman guy is pretty good --not as good as me, but still pretty good."

I ponder my options.

"Okay, it's a bet."

As if drawing a tightly strung bow, Ricky slowly pulls the stick back, moves it back and forth a couple of times, and then thrusts it forward. The cue ball kisses the rail and bumps the eight ball into the called pocket. The cue stops just short.

"Shit. Guess I owe you five bucks. Can I pay you later?"

The explosion outside – like a car backfiring – interrupts our conversation. I rush outside to the parking lot, where Ray holds his bleeding right hand in a napkin. His mangled, bloody hand looks like road kill. A crowd gathers.

"What the hell happened?" I ask.

"Nothing," Ray says.

"Nothing?"

"I just bet Hog five dollars I could carry a lit cherry bomb all the way across the parking lot before it exploded. That's all."

"Let me guess. You lost."

"That's about the size of it."

"Why did you make a dumb-ass bet like that anyway?"

"I needed the money."

Labor Day

From my perch high up in my lifeguard chair, I adjust my binoculars. The first thing I see as my field of vision shifts from fuzzy to focused is cleavage, a valley between breasts, visible above a slender black bikini bra. The breasts, about the size of the tomatoes that I would pick in our backyard garden after a rainy day, are tanned and beaded with water, and the shapes of the nipples are visible behind the bikini top. As a rule, I don't make a habit of sitting in the high chair and checking out breasts. I am supposed to be scanning the lake, looking for swimmers who might be in trouble. The breasts are just a coincidence.

Life-guarding is one of my two summer jobs. The other is pumping gas at the Redbird station out on Highway 62. The lifeguard gig is at Burdette Park Lake, a brackish saltwater pond on the far west side of Evansville, Indiana, where you stash your street clothes in a wire basket, clip a safety pin with a corresponding number on your swim trunks, and swim all afternoon for fifty cents. During the weeks leading up to Labor Day weekend, which ends the swim season, I have acquired a nice tan, and during the early part of the summer, I got in shape for football by running barefoot on the sand around the lake early in the morning. I also played American Legion baseball – first base and outfield. My hero is Roger Maris. He and Mickey Mantle are chasing Babe Ruth's season home run record. I am rooting for Maris. His two homers last night off Frank Lary and Hank Aguirre of Detroit are his 52nd and 53rd.

When I move the binoculars upward, I realize that the breasts I have been gawking at belong to Martha Mattingly, whom I have known since our days at Centennial Elementary School. When did she sprout those? Did they blossom over the summer? Or had they been there all along and I never noticed them? And those curves – they were new too. She looks good in her dark sunglasses, black bikini, and suntanned skin glistening with baby oil. I feel guilty for spying on her.

"What are you looking at, Gator?" says Ray, who often rides to work with me and joins me in my morning runs around the lake.

"Nothing in particular."

"Right. Now get down and hand me those binoculars. Your shift is over."

The first thing I do once I climb down is fire up a Marlboro. We aren't allowed to smoke on duty, but we can on break.

"I don't understand why you smoke that shit," Ray says.

FIRST DAY OF SCHOOL

The first person to greet me in Mr. Madison's homeroom is Martha Mattingly.

"Are you ready for another year of reading, writing, and arithmetic?" she asks.

"I guess so," I say, shrugging.

The 8 a.m. bell rings, and Mr. Madison, who is also the P.A. announcer at football and basketball games, reads from the daily bulletin as he does every weekday morning. His bow tie bobs up and down on his Adam's apple as he reads: *"Students will refrain from parking on Summit Avenue during school hours....A signup sheet for the fall play will be posted outside Mr. Kramer's homeroom ....Activity tickets will go on sale in homeroom beginning tomorrow.... We will be on ECA schedule throughout the first week of school....Tickets for Friday's football game vs. Muncie Central go on sale today for $2 in the athletic office. Reitz High School activity tickets will be good for the game. Come cheer the Panthers to another victory. Blah, blah, blah, blah......."*

I don't pay any attention to anything he says because I am too busy looking out the window, watching a barge round the bend of the Ohio River, plowing its muddy way toward the Mississippi. On days when the power plant isn't coughing out too much smoke, and the wind is blowing in the right direction, you can see the faint outline of Old Henderson Railroad bridge on the southern horizon just beyond the soybean fields of Union Township.

"...Students interested in NFL – that's the National Forensic League, Mr. Gates, not the National Football League – should see Mrs. Boyd..."

When he finishes reading, he wads the bulletin into a tight ball and without looking, banks a twenty-foot hook shot off the wall and into the trash can, a shot he makes about seventy percent of the time.

"Yessss!!" he says, pumping his fist.

Sometimes, with uncanny accuracy, he dusts students with chalk erasers if they are talking or daydreaming when they should be listening. When he isn't teaching journalism, Mr. Madison can usually be found chain smoking Camel unfiltereds in the teachers' lounge. During the summer, he works at the pari-mutuel window at the racetrack. His voice is soft and restrained, probably the result of thirty years of heavy smoking, but you'd never know it if you heard him announce a score over the stadium P.A. system: "TOUCHDOWN PANTHERS!!!" Mercifully, the bell rings, and we all rise from our seats and scurry off to our first-period classes.

"Going to the game this weekend?" I ask Martha.

"Maybe," she says. I had forgotten how cute her dimples are when she smiles.

THE SEASON

FIRST GAME

Ordinarily my heart would thump like the bass drums outside the field house, but sitting on the third row with the reserves and underclassmen before the game, I have a hard time giving a shit. We are getting ready to play the Muncie Central Bearcats, the top-ranked team in the state according to the pre-season polls.

Rumor had it that Coach set up the Muncie Central game in the off-season at a coach's clinic in Indianapolis. Allegedly, after all the workshops were finished, he was walking down the hall in his hotel with $100 that he was going to spend on beer and ice. His plan was to ice down the bathtub in the hotel room, fill it full of beer, and party all night. As he walked down the hall, a fragment of a conversation leaked out of a hotel room. Coach stopped by to eavesdrop. Muncie Central's coach was boasting to other coaches in the room that his Bearcats could clobber Coach Doggett's team if they ever played. Coach poked his head in and challenged his Bearcats to a two-game series, the first one on our field and then a second game in Muncie next fall. Not wanting to back down in front of his fellow coaches, Muncie's coach agreed to the two-game series. To sweeten the deal, Coach Doggett bet the Muncie Coach $100 that his Bearcats wouldn't make a first down.

"Did you see the size of those guys?" Hog asks.

"Yeah, they're big. So what? The bigger they are..."

"And all their coaches are wearing headsets with microphones."

"You're not afraid of headsets and microphones, are you?"

Coach leads the team prayer: "Our heavenly father..."

I am not listening, but it is something along these lines: *"Our heavenly Father, be with us tonight as we stomp the living shit out of these misguided sons-of-bitches who have dared to set foot on our home soil. May we squash them like sweat bees and send them back to whatever part of the state they came from with their tails dragging between their legs. In Jesus' holy name. Amen."*

I think back to a story I heard in Sunday school about Moses, who dispatched scouts into the Promised Land. When they returned with their scouting reports, most of them said, "They're huge. They'll kill us." Only Caleb and Joshua said "We can take 'em." Moses went with the majority and spent forty unnecessary years meandering around the desert.

Then Coach begins his peptic talk: "Boys, we're pretty banged up, but I think we've got a good team. Tonight we're going to find out how good. They think we're overrated, and there's nothing they'd like more than to whip the defending state champions on their own field. We have to show them what kind of football we play in this part of the state....blah, blah, blah, cuss word, cliché, blah, blah, blah.....Blah, blah, blah, cuss word, cliche, teamwork, blah, blah, pride, blah, blah, execution, blah, blah, pride, blah, block, tackle, blah, blah. Foam, foam. Now let's go kick some butt!"

Then the doors fly open, and we explode from the field house in an orgasmic burst across the tiny concrete portico, illuminated by one dim bulb, and out onto a bright green rectangle, bathed in light, untrammeled by human cleats for almost a year. We cannot be more confident had we been toting the Ark of the Covenant in front of us. Ten-thousand rabid fans stand and scream as the marching band, clad in brand new navy and gray uniforms, launch into the school song: a knockoff of the University of Wisconsin's fight song. The cheerleaders, beaming broad lipstick smiles, bounce and jiggle in the zone between the playing field and the cheering section. Two of the cheerleaders are girlfriends of our team captains. Cindy Sullivan, the only blond among a squad of brunettes, has been Donnie McDowell's steady girl for three years. Barely five feet tall and 100 pounds, she is as petite as Donnie is huge. Patty Nichols, a junior with long brown hair pulled back into a ponytail, has been Tony Reavis' since her freshman year. Out on the cinder track which loops around the field, Jill Henderson and Martha Mattingly hold up a hoop that reads "Smite the Bearcats" or something like that. Everyone races to be first through the hoop like a bunch of testosterone-crazed sperms racing to an unfertilized egg. Ray Moon crashes through first.

A cantaloupe-colored moon hovers in the early September sky, and Old Glory rests limply against the flagpole at the summit of the chute as the pep band plays the National Anthem. Tony Reavis wins the coin toss and opts to receive. The Muncie kicker's toe makes contact with the ball, and the teams charge at each other like medieval armies. Kenny Cain takes the ball on the ten and totes it out to the 34-yard line. On our first play from scrimmage, Donnie churns up the middle for three yards, carrying three Muncie tacklers with him. But an off-sides penalty brings the ball back. On the second play, Charlie takes the snap and hands to Ricky, who has taken over my backfield spot while I am in coach's doghouse. He races untouched down the right sideline for the first six points of the season.

"Touchdown! Ricky Ferrell!" roars Mr. Madison over the public address system.

I have mixed emotions. I am happy we scored, but I am beginning to wonder whether I will ever get my starting job back.

Charlie scores on a long run the next time we get the ball. Then Donnie scores on a short run. We score every time we get the ball, but even when we are up four touchdowns, I don't get into the game. From the bench, I watch the scoreboard light up. Kenny Cain scores on a reverse, and not to be outdone, his brother Benny makes a diving catch in the end zone just before halftime to put us up 33-0.

As we file into the locker room, we figure the Old Man would be pleased. We figure wrong. Coach Doggett storms in and writes "PUSSIES!" in all caps on the chalkboard.

"Moon!" he screams at Ray, who is seated on the front row with all the linemen. Backs sit on the second row. I sit on the third row with the reserves and underclassmen.

"Sir?"

"Do you know how to throw a god-damned block?"

"Yes, sir."

"Then why don't you?"

"Sir, my man is at least fifty pounds heavier than I am and my hand..."

Coach Doggett, in good shape despite his beer belly, thrusts forward, and with his forearms, knocks Ray backwards off the bench.

"That's how you throw a god-damned block, son! Can you do that?"

"Yes, sir."

"Then do it!"

Once Ray reclaims his seat, Coach grabs Ray's scarred silver helmet and whacks him on the side of the head. The blow draws blood.

"Now stop thinking about what you're going to do after the game and start thinking about what's in front of you! Is that clear?"

Ray rises from the bench and looks the Old Man straight in his bloodshot eyes. Veins pop out in Ray's neck, forehead, and his massive biceps, where Jill's name is etched in a crude homemade tattoo. His jaws and fists clench. I can tell that Ray wants more than anything to knock the Old Man backwards through the chalkboard. He can too, and Coach knows it. I think, "Shit, this is going to be interesting." Jimmy Dean's lyrics echo in my head: *Kinda broad at the shoulders, narrow at the hip. Everybody knows you don't give no lip to Big John.* Somehow Ray composes himself, deciding instead to take out his aggression on whatever unlucky bastard lines up across from him in the second half.

The second half is more of the same. I sneak into the game with the third stringers late in the fourth quarter -- time enough for me to get a penalty for piling on the Muncie ball carrier after he has been tackled. I can't resist. I just want to see some action. That penalty is the only first down the Bearcats make all evening, and it will cost Coach $100. (My indiscretion results in my running the chute a half dozen times Monday in practice.) I carry the ball once late in the fourth quarter, down at the Muncie goal line. Our third-string quarterback calls Spin 22. When I get the ball, I head toward the designated hole, but there is no opening -- our sophomores are not as good at opening holes as our seniors -- so I go airborne. I dive over the line, but just as I reach the goal line, a Muncie helmet hits me in the balls. I stagger off the field, eyes watering, trying hard not to hold my aching gonads.

We end up winning 66-0. At the end of the game, I sit quietly in the field house while my teammates crow and snap towels. My balls are as big as water balloons -- blue ones. As I tuck my shirt, a man in a plaid sport coat walks into the mayhem and finds Coach Doggett.

I recognize the man as Muncie's head coach.

"Coach, what would it take to get out of next year's game?"

"We both stand to lose a lot of money if we cancel a game," Coach says.

"Name your price."

Coach scratches his whiskers,

"I think $2,500 ought to cover it."

The Muncie coach pulls his checkbook from the inside jacket pocket and without blinking, writes a check for $2,500. The Old Man accepts the check and peels five crisp twenty-dollar bills from his money clip and hands them to the Muncie coach.

"What's this for?"

"You got your first down, didn't you?"

In another corner of the locker room, sportswriter Dick Burnside puffs on his pipe and scribbles in his reporter's notebook. He is talking to Ray Moon, still in shoulder pads, blood caked on the side of his head from where coach whacked him.

"Looks like you took a pretty good hit," Burnside says.

"Football is a rough game, sir."

A Thunder of Drums

On the last Friday night before the West Side Drive-In shuts down for the season, I sit in the back seat of the Cain brothers' Chevy with Kenny Cain and Martha Mattingly. Benny Cain sits in the front seat with Hog and an ice chest of cold beer. The movie is *A Thunder of Drums* starring Richard Boone, George Hamilton, and Slim Pickens, a run-of-the-mill Fort Apache Cavalry vs. Indians flick. Duane "Twangin' Guitar" Eddy has a small role in it.

"Hey, he was on *Have Gun Will Travel* last week," I remark.

"Richard Boone is always on *Have Gun Will Travel*. Or haven't you noticed that?"

"No. I mean Duane Eddy..."

Few people go to the drive-in to watch movies. Most go to drink beer and hang out. Some go to make out. Whatever is on the screen is unimportant and irrelevant. Martha, still wearing her pink pinstriped Parkway dress, boasts about her newly acquired brown belt in karate.

"If either of you attacked me, I could flatten you," she brags. She has already chugged a couple of beers and is working on a third.

"No you couldn't," says Kenny.

"Yes I could."

"No you couldn't."

"Go on. Try to hit me."

"I don't want to."

"Just throw a punch, OK?"

"What if I hurt you?"

"You won't hurt me. I can take care of myself."

Before she knows what hits her, Kenny lands a left hook that knocks her cold. Kenny, Benny, Hog, and I look at each other for a few puzzled seconds before anyone can think of anything to say or do. I consider popping Kenny in the face, but I don't. After all, Martha did ask for it. Hog finally breaks the silence.

"You dumb ass! Look what you've done!"

"Shit. I'm sorry!"

"What do we do now?"

"I don't know."

We do nothing. Martha, who has fallen across my lap, doesn't revive until midway through *The Guns of Navarrone*. (The guns wake her, I think.) Her right eye is swollen shut and the tissue surrounding it has turned a ghastly shade of purple.

"What happened?"

"Kenny hit you."

"Oh," she says groggily. "Can I have a beer?"

Hog fishes a cold one from the cooler and hands it to her. For the rest of the night, when Martha isn't swilling cold Sterling, she presses the ice-cold can against her bruised face.

Repentance

St. Paul's Methodist Church is hot as hell the second Sunday in September. The congregation fans themselves with paper fans that have a picture of Jesus holding a lost lamb on one side and an advertisement for the Johnson

Funeral Home, which is operated by Hog's uncle, on the other. (I suppose if someone died of heat stroke, we would know where to take that person.)

"Emmanuel. God is with us. I'm as certain of that as I'm certain that organ is going to play when it's time for the next hymn," Dad proclaims joyfully and confidently from the pulpit. My father is the lay leader there – and he often leads Sunday services when Rev. Chappell is on vacation. (Church was part of my upbringing. I was baptized when I was a month old and confirmed when I was in the sixth grade, and almost every Sunday morning of my life, Mom and Dad would drag me to Sunday school and church for a healthy dose of Jesus.) I squirm in the pew and fidget with my too-tight neck tie. I am hung over big time, my head aches, and I feel a little guilty and repentant about my behavior of the previous night. But then I think about Dad's stash of Sterlings in the fallout shelter's fridge. Beer is a necessity in the event of nuclear attack, Dad rationalizes. Or just about any other occasion that might arise, for that matter.

Every Sunday is the same old ritual: call to worship, welcome, announcements, Lord's Prayer, three ponderous 19th-century hymns, scripture reading, offering, sermon, closing remarks, doxology, etc...But when it is time for the closing hymn, the organ remains mute. Apparently everyone on the West Side has cranked up their air conditioners, and the power blows out all over the West Side. Our organist, a middle-aged lady with excessively rouged cheeks, shrugs. Dad mops his big bald head with a handkerchief and ad-libs something about God's wry sense of humor. We close with an *a capella* version of "Faith of Our Fathers." After the benediction – *May the Lord bless you and keep you and be gracious unto you. May the Lord make his face to shine upon you etc....* I burst through the heavy oak doors, not unlike the way I burst through the field house doors two nights before. The sun smacks me in the face and drops me to my knees like Saul on the way to Damascus. Shielding my eyes, I make my way to the bushes and purge the beer from the night before. Jesus is not pleased.

After church and a big Sunday dinner, I retire to the living room in time to watch Roger Maris hit home run number 61 off Boston's Tracy Stallard in the last game of the season.

CENTRAL

The Central locker room is cold and cramped with paper-thin walls. Kenny Cain, sits on a bench listening to game one of the World Series on his transistor radio while his teammates put on their blue road uniforms. We won our first three games, all at home – 66-0 against Muncie

Central, 53-0 vs. Crawfordsville, and 42-0 vs. Mater Dei. Central's Bears would be our first road test. Dick Burnside had written in the Sunday Courier that we were good enough to go through the season without allowing a point. Some of us are thinking about Burnside's challenge, but we do not talk about it. Even though we had whipped everybody we played, I never saw any action until late in the games when the reserves and underclassmen were mopping up. Clearly, I am still in coach's doghouse, and I am not sure when or how I will get out of it.

"Who's winning?" I ask.

Kenny removes his earphone.

"Who's winning?" I repeat.

"Yankees, 2-0."

Kenny puts the earphone back in his ear as Coach Doggett enters the locker room.

"Gather 'round boys," he grunts.

We squeeze together on three long benches, linemen on the front row, backs and receivers on the second, and reserves and underclassmen on the third row. Those who cannot find room on the benches sit on their helmets or lean against lockers.

"There's been some talk in the newspapers about us going through a season without allowing a point," Coach begins. "That's never been done, and I want to be the first one to do it."

He pops an antacid and before long the foaming starts.

"Boys, this is going to be our toughest game so far. We're going to be playing on a foreign field in front of a hostile crowd, and we're playing a good team….." Then he notices Kenny's earphones.

"Cain!!" He is not sure whether he was talking to Kenny or Benny.

Kenny removes his earphones.

"Sir?"

"Who is winning?"

"Yanks 2-0"

"Perhaps you would be so kind as to let us all listen to the game."

Kenny unplugs the phones, and we huddle around the radio as Mel Allen calls the top of the ninth inning. Whitey Ford gets Vada Pinson, Wally Post, and Frank Robinson to ground out, fly out, and strike out in consecutive at-bats, giving the Yankees a 2-0 win and a 1-0 series lead. Going back to the 1960 Series against the Pirates, the Yankee left-hander has racked up twenty-seven consecutive scoreless innings, a post-season record.

"That's three straight shutouts," Coach Doggett says. "Whitey Ford's got nothing on us. Let's get a fourth one tonight. What do you say?"

"Yes, sir!" we all shout.

Then he resumes his pre-game talk, which is essentially the same one we had heard dozens of times: "blocking…. tackling…teamwork….execution….cuss word, cuss word, cuss word, cliché, cliché, cliché… pride….dedication,….. toughness…." Coach continues. "Now let's get out there and beat the ever-loving crap out of these guys."

"Yes, sir!!"

As Kenny makes his way toward the exit, helmet in hand, Coach smashes him on top of his crew-cut with his clipboard.

"That's for listening to the ballgame when I'm talking."

From the opening series of downs, it is clear that something is not right with Kenny. When he breaks from the huddle, Kenny lines up in the wrong position, and Charlie has to move him to right spot. When the ball is snapped, Kenny misses his blocking assignment as a Central tackler shoots through a gap in the line to stop Donnie for no gain. Coach sends in the next play, the reverse that Kenny scored on in the first game of the season.

Once again, Charlie points Kenny to the right spot, but at the snap, Kenny runs headlong into the line instead of coming back for the ball. Charlie has to keep it and gets sacked for a three-yard loss. After the play, Charlie trots to the sidelines.

"Coach," he pleads. "You've got to get Kenny out of the lineup. He's lost out there. He doesn't look right. His eyes look funny and he keeps saying 'What do I do? What do I do?'"

Coach looks down the bench at me and scratches the bristles on his chin as he weighs his options. I think that, with a little luck, I might get in the game early, and if I perform well, I might even get back into the starting lineup. But Coach keeps Kenny in the game and doesn't yank him until early in the second quarter, when it is clear that Kenny is clueless. By that time, we have gone three and out three times. Fortunately, Central isn't moving the ball any better. We take turns punting and playing between the 30-yard-lines, battling for control of the middle of the field like men on a chessboard.

With the score knotted at 0-0 and Central steadily moving the ball down the field, Coach glares at me from under the brim of his gray fedora and motions me into the game.

"Go in for Cain at cornerback," he growls.

As I hustle onto the field, I pass Kenny as he jogs toward the sidelines. His eyes are glazed and unfocused.

"Are you all right, man?" I ask.

"Who are you?" he says.

When the teams break from their huddles, I line up at right corner, a few yards behind Ray at tackle and Hog at defensive end. At the far end of the field, our fans stand on rickety wooden bleachers under an old sycamore tree and cheer while the cheerleaders go through their routines. *"Push 'em back, push 'em back. Way back...."*

Ray talks trash to Central's tight end, a 250-pound colored kid who lines up across from Hog. The ball is at midfield.

"Who's your daddy?" Ray taunts.

We don't have any black players on our team. Back when I was a sophomore, a black kid from the Hillcrest Orphanage went out for the team, but he quit after a couple of weeks because we made life so hard for him. Back in those days, all of Evansville west of Pigeon Creek was lily white. It still is.

When the ball is snapped, the black kid flattens Hog like a Styrofoam cup, and Central quarterback Rex Humphries (who would later become a district judge) takes off around right end. With Hog out of the way, Humphries turns the corner and races down the sidelines with me and the rest of our defensive backfield in pursuit. At the nine yard line Benny Cain, racing in from his left cornerback slot, and Tony Reavis cut off angle to the end zone. I pursue from my corner spot. We all meet and drive Humphries out of bounds at the far end of the Central bench. Even though I hit him after he is out of bounds, it still feels good to make a tackle. Tony, Benny, and I get up, but Humphries remains on the ground. His eyes look a whole lot like Kenny's did when I first entered the game. The back judge tosses a flag at my feet.

"Personal foul. Half the distance to the goal line!"

The team trainer and physician race to the fallen player while we retreat to our defensive huddle.

"Goddamn it Ray! Stop talking that trash!" Hog complains. "My man is beating the shit out of me on every play."

"Take it easy," Ray says. "I'm just trying to get inside his head."

"He outweighs me by almost 100 pounds. You make him mad and he takes it out on me. Shit, get inside your own man's head!"

"Don't worry about it," Ray says. "I'll take care of it."

Eventually an ambulance arrives, and a team of EMTs carry the fallen Central quarterback off the field in a stretcher, and the game resumes with the ball at first and goal on our four-yard line, the closest anyone has been to our goal line all year.

"Dig in, guys," Tony says.

Tony is genetically predestined to be a defensive lineman. Back in '44 when Tony was still shitting yellow, his dad lost two toes on a bitter cold night in Ardennes Forest, trying to halt the coordinated advance of three German armies through allied lines, which had been stretched perilously thin. The line ruptured, but it did not hemorrhage, and thus the Battle of the Bulge goes down as perhaps history's best example of a defense that would bend but not break.

Three straight running plays net the Bears two yards. On fourth down, Tony breaks through the Bear line, runs down the backup quarterback as he rolls out to pass, and drops him for a five-yard loss. We take over at our own seven yard-line, ninety-three yards from pay dirt, six minutes from halftime.

"All right, guys. Let's put some points on the board," Charlie says.

Slowly we press forward in three or four yard chunks with Donnie picking up most of the tough yardage, dragging tacklers the way a blue ribbon tractor at the county fair keeps surging forward no matter how many boys hop on the sled towed behind it. Coach doesn't really buy into Woody Hayes' three yards and a cloud of dust theory. He prefers to score from long distance. Yards come tougher the closer we get to the end zone, he believes. But we aren't breaking any long runs. And the Bears obviously watched game film of the reverse play that had worked so well in our first three games.

On the Bear thirty-three yard line with thirty seconds left in the half, Charlie calls a pass play. As a rule, we only pass seven or eight times a game, usually against a defense stacked tight to guard against the run. We only have a handful of pass plays in our playbook, some of them old school jump passes to receivers slanting over the middle of the field between the linebackers and the defensive secondary. Charlie's favorite, though, is to fake the ball to one of his wingbacks, then drop back and heave the ball as far as he can, usually to one of the twins, who could run down almost any pass thrown in their direction.

"Fly 44 left," Charlie barks.

"What's that?" I ask. During my time on the bench, I have forgotten some of our pass plays. Charlie rolls his eyes.

"Just run like hell down the sidelines and catch it."

We clap, break from the huddle, and line up. At the signal, Hog snaps the ball back to Charlie, who fakes a handoff to Donnie plunging into the middle of the line. The fake freezes the linebackers and cornerback, and Charlie drops back and lofts a beautiful rainbow pass, which I catch in stride, and I run full speed ahead toward the end zone. Kenny or Benny would have made it easily, but Central's free safety runs me down at the one-yard line with only a few ticks left before halftime.

In the huddle, Charlie looks me in the eye and says "Spin-22, right."

We break from the huddle and line up a yard from the Bear goal line. Charlie barks the signals. On the snap count, Charlie gets the ball and hands it to me. I take dead aim at the designated hole, which opens just wide enough for me to slither through, like a cat through a screen door about to close.

"Touchdown! Russell Gates!" screams Mr. Madison.

Donnie misses the extra point and we hobble into the locker room with a shaky 6-0 lead.

We wait in the Central locker room for Coach, but he never comes in. We figure he is outside smoking a cigarette. Or maybe he is so pissed that he doesn't want to see us. The walls of the Central locker room are paper-thin and you can hear everything on the other side of the lockers. Since Coach is not around to chew us out, there is nothing to do but sit and listen to Central coach Dan Houston's halftime talk on the other side of the wall. Houston, who has a reputation of being even meaner than Coach Doggett, is hopping mad: "You bunch of pussies! They're making you look like fools out there! If you guys don't block and tackle any better than that the second half, you don't deserve to win! They're out-hitting you! They're out-hustling you! They're out-thinking you! And they're showing more heart than you! And more guts! Blah, blah, blah...

"...Shit, you men are every bit as good as they are! Hell, you're BETTER than they are! When are you going to start playing like it? How about playing like men? Have you no pride in yourselves? Have you no pride in your school? Are you going to let them kick your sorry asses all over our field? Are you going to let them take out our leader without putting up a fight? We're still in this game, boys. Our defense has been great, but we've got to figure a way to get some points on the board. Our starting quarterback is gone. We've got to pull together. We've got to block and tackle and play defense the way we're capable......Now let's go out there in the second half and WIN this game. What do you say, men?"

"Yes, sir!!" roar the Bears in unison.

"Everything you just heard goes for me too," says Coach Doggett, who has slipped into the locker room unnoticed somewhere in the middle of the Central coach's halftime oratory.

"Now let's go play some football, boys," he says calmly, and that is the extent of his halftime talk.

Ricky takes the second-half kickoff and heads straight up the middle of the field. He makes it almost all the way to midfield when a host of Bears swarms on him, and Ricky coughs up the ball. Players from both teams dive for it. When the players get off the pile, Benny Cain has the football, and the big colored boy who had given Hog fits in the first half lies motionless on the turf. While the team trainers come out to midfield, we retreat to our huddle. Ray winks at Hog.

"Told you I'd take care of it," he says.

Charlie calls the play quickly: "Spin 22 left." We break from the huddle and wait for the EMTs to carry the big colored kid off the field.

I wait in the backfield as Charlie barks the signals. Suddenly everything explodes like balls on a billiard table. Hog snaps the ball to Charlie, who pivots and hands it to me circling behind him. I race toward a hole Ray has ripped open on the left side of the line and charge through it. I pick up two or three yards when a Bear linebacker hits me helmet to helmet, and everything fades to black.

When I wake up in the hospital room, Ray and Ricky are seated at the foot of my bed. Ray tosses me a bag of clothes.

"Here. I thought you might need these," he says.

"Shit. Where am I? What happened?" I say.

"Concussion," Ray says. "You took a wicked hit, man."

"Did we win?"

"Yup. 21-0. We're still undefeated, untied, and unscored on."

Flyboy

I sit at a booth at Parkway with Tony Reavis and Patty Nichols. I'm chomping on a cheeseburger while Tony and Patty look through some brochures from the United States Air Force Academy. More than a dozen colleges have been courting Tony, the Air Force Academy more aggressively than most.

"Look at this place!" exclaims Tony. Underneath a photograph of the academy's spired chapel is a photo of the interior of Arnold Hall with its polished marble floor and elegant spiral staircases.

"Jeez, this looks like a five-star hotel," he says.

"And look!" he says, pointing to a photograph of the academy's brand new 40,000 seat Falcon Stadium. "This would be a cool place to play."

"Listen to this," says Patty. "They have girls on staff who are assigned to date dateless cadets."

"Wow!" I say. "If you go to school there, you'll have it made, dude."

Patty frowns.

"I don't much care for it," she says.

"I don't either," says Tony. "All I want to do is fly and maybe play some football."

The Edict

Every year during the first week of October, just as the leaves change color and the air grows cooler, the Miller Amusement Company sets up its Ferris wheel, merry-go-round, Scrambler, Tilt-a-Whirl, Bullet, and other rides and midway attractions on the public library lawn, and scores of civic organizations and churches erect booths up and down Franklin Street, where they hawk brain sandwiches, bratwursts, pronto pups, sausage burgers, funnel cakes, and other deep-fried confections to fairgoers who have never heard of cholesterol and could care less about counting calories. The second largest street fair in North America after Mardi Gras, the annual West Side Fall Festival, in Coach's opinion, offers too many distractions and temptations for seventeen-year-old boys who ought to be focused on football.

Our next opponent would be the New Albany Bulldogs, and we would be playing them on their field. The Bulldogs are 3-1, their only loss coming at the hands of Central early in the season.

"If I catch any of you boys on Franklin Street this week, you will not suit up for the New Albany game," Coach warns us at Monday afternoon's practice. I assume I am exempt from his edict since Doc Jenkins, our team physician, has grounded me for at least a week as a result of the concussion I received in the Central game. Doc, who easily weighs 350 pounds, played on the line for Coach back in the early '50s. He is also on the Fall Festival board, and he has probably consumed more deep-fried food over the years than our whole team combined.

"Why does the Old Man get to go and we don't?" whispers Ray.

"Same reason he keeps the field watered while we go thirsty."

"That's not fair!"

"Shit, life isn't fair. Or haven't you figured that out yet?"

"Moon, Gates!!!!" barks the Old Man.

"Yes, sir!!!"

"Do you have something to share?"

"No, sir!!!"

"Then stop running your mouth and start running the chute! The rest of you hit the showers and stay away from Franklin Street!"

"Yes, sir!!" everyone shouts.

Once everyone is in the field house, Coach and Doc head toward Franklin Street to meet their wives. Ray and I commence chugging up the hill.

"So are you going?" Ray huffs.

"Going where?"

"Franklin Street."

"I don't know. I'm already in deep shit. What about you?"

"Hell yes, I'm going. Hey, have you got a date for Homecoming, Gator?"

"Sorry Ray. I'm already taken."

"Who are you going with?"

"Nobody you know."

"Nobody period. You ought to ask Martha Mattingly. She likes you, man. Damned if I know why. She's not half bad looking either. You might even get a little, if you know what I mean. Just think about it."

"I'll think about it."

HOME

After I finish showering, I walk home to our little brownstone bungalow on the south side of Reitz Hill. Mom and Dad are seated in the living room, watching the evening news on a black and white RCA console TV. We have three channels, and the remote control has not been invented. Dad fiddles with the rabbit ear antenna while Walter Cronkite talks about how President Kennedy is sending Gen. Maxwell Taylor on a fact-finding mission to someplace called Vietnam.

"Where the hell is Vietnam?" Dad mumbles.

"Someplace in Asia, I think."

"We left your supper in the kitchen," Mom says.

The only things on the table that came from the grocery store are a platter of fried chicken and a pitcher of sweet iced tea. Everything else comes from our back yard garden – sliced tomatoes, sweet corn, green beans and new potatoes, sliced watermelon. Mom loves to cook and she loves to can vegetables. Every summer she preserves veggies in Mason jars and stores them in our root cellar grotto dug into the hillside. Like many folks who were sure the Russians were going to drop a nuclear bomb on us any day, Dad converted our root cellar to a fallout shelter, complete with cots, folding chairs, short-wave radio, a refrigerator full of beer, and shelves loaded with Mason jars filled with fruits and vegetables – apples, peaches, beans, corn, cucumbers, okra. They remind me of the specimen jars in Mr. Grayson's biology class. I fill my plate up twice and go to the bathroom to weigh myself. I weigh 165 pounds, which is what I always weigh after practice, plus or minus a pound or two, even after eating enough food for two people.

Gunsmoke is on when I return to the living room.

"Dad, can I borrow the car?" I ask.

"You know the rules," Dad says. "Not on a week night."

"Can I get a motorcycle?"

"If you go through the whole season without giving up a point, I'll get you a motorcycle."

"Seriously?"

"Maybe."

Dad played tailback for Coach Doggett back in the '40s. He was also the team's punter and placekicker. Twenty years later he is a route driver for a potato chip company.

"Why were you late tonight?" Dad says.

"I had to run the chute."

Dad smiles.

"Back when I played, I probably had to run that chute a hundred times," Dad says. He is always eager to reminisce about his glory days.

"Yeah, yeah, yeah. All in one day, right?"

I plop in the recliner and pick up the afternoon Press to see what was going to be on TV that night – *Maverick, Twilight Zone, Leave It to Beaver*...

"You know the rules, Russell," Mom says. "No TV until your homework is done."

I retreat to my room and open my history textbook to the chapter about the Civil War when I hear the rapping at the window. I go to the window and open it.

"Let's go to Franklin Street," whispers Kenny Cain, standing in our rose bushes. His transistor radio is in his shirt pocket, and the earphone is deep in his ear canal. His breath smells of beer.

"I've got homework."

"So do I. Come on. We'll only be gone an hour or so. Nobody will know."

"Where's Benny?"

"He's studying for the same history test you're studying for."

That makes sense. If there is a difference between the twins, it is that Kenny is the more outgoing of the two. He likes to party, whereas Benny mostly keeps to himself. During our junior year, Kenny had a small speaking role in the drama department's production of *Mr. Roberts*. Benny ran the lights.

"Let's go, Gator," Kenny says. "You can study when you get back. Shit, I can tell you who won the war."

FALL FESTIVAL

From the top of the Ferris wheel, you can see the vendors' booths stretching all the way down Franklin Street to St. Joseph Avenue. We climb ten or fifteen feet, and our gondola swings as riders get off and new riders board. The maple leaves at treetop level are bright orange. The four of us – Martha Mattingly, Kenny Cain, me, and a goldfish in a plastic bag that I won on the midway -- are going to be there for a while. Kenny listens to game three of the World Series on his earphones. On the stage across the street, twin girls, dressed as convicts and chained at the ankles, play accordions, tap-dance, and sing as people stroll past munching on corn dogs, candy apples, and other foodstuffs on sticks. Martha, who a few minutes before had run into Kenny and me on the midway where we had been tossing ping pong balls into goldfish bowls, is wedged tightly between us, munching on a corn dog.

"Have you asked anyone to Homecoming?" she asks.

"Not yet," I say.

"Homecoming is in two weeks, you know."

"That soon?"

I am terrified of heights, and the Ferris wheel scares me more than any ride in the carnival, including the roller coaster. I grab the safety bar on the gondola and white-knuckle it for dear life. When I see Coach Doggett and his wife Louise walking on the midway far below, I slump down in the seat.

"You're not afraid of him, are you?" she says.

"Terrified."

"What can he do to you? Keep you from playing? You're not playing Friday anyway."

"If he caught me here with a girl, he could kick me off the team."

"That's stupid."

"Yes, it's stupid, but Coach doesn't allow dating during the season."

"We're not dating."

Martha is editor of the school paper, among other things. She probably has more ink under her yearbook picture than anyone in my senior class. And once you get past her black cat-eye glasses, she is not bad looking. Her brown hair is pulled back into a ponytail, and she carries the world's largest purse.

Kenny produces a pack of Winstons, takes one for himself, and offers smokes to Martha and me. Martha accepts and lights up as do I. From the depths of her cavernous purse, Martha produces a shiny flask of peppermint schnapps, takes a long pull, and passes it around. Kenny takes a swig and passes it to me. I follow suit.

Far below Ray, wearing his navy blue letter sweater with a big gray "R" emblazoned across his chest and wielding a heavy sledge hammer, stands at the test your strength booth on the street corner with Jill, who clutches a large stuffed bear which Ray has won for her on the midway. The crowd swirls around them like floodwaters in a swollen creek. I want to throw something, but all I have is a plastic bag with a fish in it.

"Don't!" Martha pleads.

Too late. I loft my fish grenade and watch in awe as it plummets to earth, landing about six feet from Ray and Jill, splattering everybody within twenty-five feet of ground zero, including the booth's operator, a surly-looking man with dark skin and tattooed forearms.

"Who did that???" he shouts, looking up at the Ferris wheel, using his hand to shield his eyes. "I'll tear you a new asshole whoever you are!"

I shrink back in the gondola. Martha looks horrified.

"Did you want that fish?" I ask. "I can win you another one."

"You're an idiot," she says. If the Ferris wheel were a car at an intersection, she would get out and walk.

"Would you guys shut up?" Kenny shouts, louder than he needs to. "Roger Maris is up in the top of the ninth. Score is tied 2-2."

"Pull that damned earphone out so we can listen," I say.

"Funny, isn't it? Yanks and Reds," says Martha.

"What do you mean?" Kenny says.

"Didn't you see this morning's paper?"

"Only the sports page."

"The Russians just exploded a hydrogen bomb yesterday, and we're going to be testing a bigger one tomorrow."

"So? What's that have to do with the price of beans in Russia?"

"Yanks and Reds, man. That's Cold War irony. Don't you guys get it? Think about it: Yanks and Reds."

"Sssssshhhh!!!" Kenny says.

From the top of the Ferris wheel, we listen as Maris knocks a Bob Purkey knuckleball into the right-field bleachers of Crosley Field to give the Yankees a 3-2 lead. Luis Arroyo holds the Reds scoreless in the bottom of the ninth, preserving the victory and giving the Yankees a 2-1 series lead.

HOME AGAIN

On the way home, Kenny runs his car, an old beater he and Benny bought from an uncle for $100, into a utility pole a few blocks from my house. In addition to being snockered on schnapps, Kenny has been drinking beer. Kenny likes to drink. He also likes to drive. When the twins are together, more often than not, Kenny is the one behind the wheel. I offered to drive, but Kenny declined.

Nobody is hurt, and the car is still drivable, but the impact leaves a noticeable crease in the front bumper and grille.

"Think Benny will notice that?" he asks.

"Probably."

Kenny puts the car in reverse and backs into the street. I get out before he can put the car in drive.

"I'll walk from here," I say.

"You sure? It's no trouble."

"Yeah, I'm sure. Maybe you'd better walk too. Schnapps and hops don't mix."

"Nah, I'm good."

"See you tomorrow."

His tires squeal as he stomps the accelerator. I walk home the last three blocks and slither through my bedroom window, which I had propped open with my history book. Once back in the house, I tiptoe to the bathroom, lean over the toilet, and puke up everything I had on Franklin Street. Then I tiptoe back to my room, flop in bed, and fall asleep, and dream that my old man has grabbed me by the hair and is beating me across the face while my mother sobs at the threshold to my room. When I go down to breakfast in the morning, I learn that I had not been dreaming. Mom and Dad are waiting. Mom is still sobbing. They ground me for the rest of the semester. No more access to the family car. No leaving the house after school except for work and football. If my old man hadn't played football back in his day, he would have forbidden that too. But he wants to relive his glory days on the gridiron vicariously through me, I think. What really sucks is that my concussion is going to ground me for at least one football game in addition to my grounding at home. Head hurting badly, I walk to school and flunk a second-period history test over the Civil War.

Hit the Road, Jack

New Albany, Indiana, is about 120 miles upriver from Evansville, right across the Ohio River from Louisville.

The New Albany Bulldogs are 4-0, and they badly want to beat us. The Bulldogs hadn't crossed our goal line in three years. The year before, we thrashed them 34-0 at our place, and they desperately want to return the favor. We all get out of school in the middle of the afternoon to make the two-hour road trip through the wooded hills of southern Indiana. Some of the guys play clabber or poker. Others nap or listen to the World Series on the radio. I pass time reading the *Mirror*, our student newspaper. On the sports page, in Martha Mattingly's account of our win over Central, the headline reads "Panthers Route Bears 21-0." The misspelling bothers me. "Where the hell did we route them?" I wonder. When I finish reading the paper, I stare out the window at fields of brown, brittle cornrows and long stretches of woods whose leaves had, only within the last few days, combusted into brilliant shades of red, gold, orange, and yellow.

We get to the field around 6 p.m. and file into the visitors' locker room, where we change from our street clothes into our blue road uniforms. Once dressed for battle, we assemble as we always do: seniors and linemen on the front row, backs on the second row, reserves and underclassmen on the back rows. I dress even though I know I won't play.

Coach begins his talk: "Boys, we've played four games, and we haven't given up a point. This team wants to be the first team to score on us, and they want to be the first team to beat us......"

While Coach rants, Hog chugs an elixir made of honey and raw eggs that he had concocted at home and brought along in a canteen. The drink, he believes, gives him a boost both in energy and in calories. Hog, our offensive center and defensive end, weighs barely 170 pounds. He earned the nickname Hog, not because he was fat, but because he loved to play in the mud. Back in our freshman year, we scrimmaged one afternoon in a driving rain, and the practice field, which was ordinarily a dust bowl, quickly turned into a soupy, muddy wallow. Hog got his face driven into the mud on almost every play. Once when he got back to our huddle, greasy with mud from helmet to cleats, Charlie said "Damn, Johnson. You look like one of my uncle's hogs that's been wallowing in a mud hole. And you don't smell so good either." The name stuck, and almost every week Richard "Hog" Johnson found himself lining up against players thirty to forty pounds heavier than he was, both on offense and defense. He badly wants to be bigger, but no matter how much he eats or drinks, his weight always seems to settle at around 170 pounds.

"All right, men. Let's go!"

"Yes, sir!!"

On the opening kickoff, energized from his miracle beverage, Hog takes dead aim at his man, who weighs at least 280 pounds, and charges him like Crazy Horse. When they meet at midfield, the big kid does something Hog doesn't expect: He goes low and sends Hog somersaulting in the air and belly flopping to the turf. Hog wobbles to his feet, staggers back to the huddle, and pukes. The team breaks huddle quickly.

I watch the game from the bench – doctor's orders.

It is a pretty good game. A light rain starts falling in the second half, and it escalates into a full-blown monsoon by the third quarter, just the kind of game Hog loves. We win 26-0, and Ray gets his first and only varsity touchdown in the fourth quarter when he rushes the passer, tips the ball as it leaves the quarterback's hand, catches it in stride, and lumbers into the end zone. Everyone on the team piles on him. I would have too, had I been on the field.

On the way home, the rain falls in thick sheets, and lightning flashes to the south as the team bus weaves its way back to Evansville. Midway home, we stop at a truck stop in Dale, Indiana, for fuel and food. The student bus – about forty made the trip to New Albany to sit in the rain on rickety bleachers on the far end of the field -- is already parked there, next to a pickup truck loaded with watermelons. We are wringing wet when we get inside the diner. As soon as we walk in, someone starts singing the school song, and everybody joins in. Then somebody starts singing "Michael, Row the Boat Ashore."

Martha is among them.

"Did you read my article about the Central game?" she asks.

"Yeah, I read it."

"Well?"

"Who wrote the headline?"

"I did. Why?"

"It said 'Panthers Route Bears.'"

"So?"

"It should have been 'rout.' Not 'route' with an 'e.' Where did we route them anyway?"

"Is that all you have to say about it?"

"No. You said our new road uniforms looked 'just darling.' Never, ever use the word 'darling' in a sports article."

"If you're so darned smart, why don't you just write up tonight's game?"

"Maybe I will."

Somewhere during the sing-along, Ray slips out. I know he isn't taking a cigarette break because Ray hates cigarettes, and he can't understand why anyone would spend good money to trash out their lungs. Where he went and what he did become apparent when the team gets back on the bus. Under the back seat are three fat watermelons.

On the drive back to Evansville, we pass the time playing poker, staring out the window, talking about girls and sports, snoozing, and eating poached watermelon.

Exile

In a pitch-black classroom, we sit and watch film of last year's game with Bloomington, our next opponent. Ray, whose only yearbook accolade besides varsity football is Projectionist Club, operates the projector. Coach Doggett is out of the room.

The teams line up. The Bloomington quarterback hands to a running back trying to sweep around end. The left side of our line and our secondary swarms him and stops him for no gain. Hog piles on after the whistle, and the back judge tosses his flag.

Ray runs the reel in reverse. Players leap off the pile, scurry chaotically to their positions, and then backwards to their huddles. He replays the play, this time in fast motion. I launch into my vocal impersonation of the Coach Doggett. I can mimic Coach pretty well, and the fact that my voice is at least an octave higher than Coach Doggett's makes it all the funnier.

"Goddam it, Johnson!" I snap. "What the hell do you think you're doing? Can't you see the goddam play is over? Get down right now and give me two million pushups, and when you're through with that, run the chute ten-thousand times!!!"

Everybody roars, and Ray laughs so hard he almost falls out of his seat. Suddenly the door opens, and a shaft of light falls across the room. We hear the footsteps, smell the after shave lotion. An elongated shadow falls across the light. The laughter stops.

"Moon!" Coach hisses.

"Yes, sir?"

"Do you think football is supposed to be fun?"

"No sir!" Ray answers. To have answered otherwise would have invited getting hit over the head with a clipboard.

"What about you Gates? Do you think football is supposed to be fun?"

What I say changes the course of my life. I don't know why I blurt it out without thinking of the consequences.

"Yes, sir. I do. But it's not fun any more."

My response catches the old man off guard. He sputters for a second or two before he speaks: "Then why don't you just quit?"

I slowly rise from my seat and walk toward the door.

"Winners never quit, Gates!" Coach shouts.

I do not look back.

"Don't forget to turn in your equipment, loser!!"

The shadows that fall across his face make him look especially sinister, like he is the heavy in a noir film.

"If any of you boys think football is supposed to be fun, you can follow Gates," Coach growls. Everyone stays put. I walk out of the field house across the concrete portico I have crossed hundreds of times before, stare into the sunlight, and squint.

"OK, God, what do I do now?" I ask. It is a rhetorical question, and I do not really expect an answer, but I get one. The voice comes from above and behind me. I turn, shield my eyes, and look up into the bleachers, where Martha Mattingly sits about ten rows up. Her instructions are clear: "Give me 350 words on the New Albany game by tomorrow afternoon."

GAS STATION

I am working at the Red Bird station on Division Street when the big blue De Soto pulls up to the pump. The tinted power windows roll down, and inside is Martha in her cat-eye sunglasses and a shade of lipstick somewhere between pink and red but leaning toward the red zone. "Runaround Sue" blasts from her radio.

"Fill 'er up, premium."

"Yes, ma'am."

I insert the hose into her gas tank, turn on the pump, and squeeze the trigger. While the pump hums, I drag the squeegee across the windshield. Then I pop her hood and check the oil – a service I ordinarily do not perform unless a customer specifically asks for it. I work at the gas station part time to save money to get a motorcycle, an American bike, not one of those new Japanese rice burners.

"Can I check your tire pressure?"

"Whatever floats your boat."

Wearing a greasy blue shirt with "Gator" on the pocket and holding an oily rag and dipstick, I feel embarrassed and even a little vulnerable. A few years before, a man named Leslie Irvin shot and killed a service station attendant here on the west side. Irvin later escaped from jail and fled to California where he got caught trying to pawn some hot merchandise. I just try to do my job and not think about things like that.

"What time do you get off?" she asks.

"In about a half-hour."

"Why don't you knock off early, and we can go riding around?"

"I can't tonight. I'm grounded."

"Do you have a date for Homecoming?"

"Not yet."

"Would you like to go with me?"

"Sure. If I can get out of house arrest."

"Your article on the New Albany game was good. Can you write up the Bloomington game?"

"Sure."

I wipe the dipstick clean, thrust it back into its scabbard, and yank it out like Arthur liberating Excalibur from its stone. The oil level is OK. The pump stops humming and the meter stops on $4.25. She hands me a five, and I hand her three quarters from the change-making gadget I wear on my belt.

"Come on, Gator. Sure you don't want to go for a ride when you get off work?"

I stand for a moment holding the hose, which is still dripping.

"No. I'd better not. I'm in enough trouble."

"Suits yourself."

Martha's tinted window rolls up, and the big blue De Soto pulls away from the pump, leaving a patch of burned rubber on the pavement as she squeals away. I think about Ricky Ferrell and his 20-year old girlfriend robbing that filling station – or liquor store – last summer. It is probably the same kind of deal: he's working and his girlfriend drives up and says "Hey, Ricky, let's go for a ride," and he says "OK what the fuck" and opens the cash register and pockets the day's receipts. They load up on beer and cigarettes and hightail it across the state line. They turn down a dirt road and park where the road dead-ends at the river. State troopers converge on them. She gets probation. Ricky gets a year in the juvenile detention center. That's the way I imagine it anyway.

HOMECOMING

For the first time in three years, I am attending a varsity football game as a spectator. No longer a member of the team, I sit in the cheering section with Martha, who looks stunning in her blue chiffon dress. I wear a rented tuxedo that is a little too snug.

Down on the track, the cheerleaders run through their routines: *"Two bits, four bits, six bits a dollar. All for Panthers, stand up and holler.......We've got a coach. We've got a team. We've got pep. And plenty of steam...."*

Cheering is difficult since I am looking at the game as a journalist. I admit, I like seeing my byline almost as much as I liked seeing my name in the box scores. I keep a small notebook and pencil inside my jacket pocket. Still, it feels awkward to experience a football game from the stands instead of the playing field. Martha squeezes my hand.

"You wish you were out there, don't you?" she asks.

"Yeah. I do," I admit. My football uniform – helmet, pads, jersey, pants, cleats – feels more comfortable than a tuxedo, too-tight shoes, and a constricting necktie. If I had a choice, I would have preferred to get smelly and dirty and nasty among a bunch of guys on the field than squirm in the bleachers with a pretty girl.

Our opponent is the Bloomington Jaguars. They are only 4-3 and no one thinks they will give us much of a game – except the Bloomington Jaguars. When they get the opening kickoff, they begin a long march downfield, mixing short runs and short passes. Midway through the first quarter, they have moved the ball first and goal on our four yard line, the deepest anyone has penetrated into our territory all season.

On first down, the defense drops the Bloomington fullback for no gain. When the players unpile, Donnie McDowell writhes on the turf, holding his knee. The cheering section lets out a collective gasp and then goes silent as Doc Jenkins and the team trainer stride to midfield. After a few minutes, the Cain twins help Donnie to his feet and assist him to the sidelines and into the locker room. Cindy stops cheering and watches as her boyfriend is escorted from the field. Play resumes. When the Jaguars break from the huddle, Ricky creeps up from his free safety spot to fill Donnie's middle linebacker position.

On second and goal, the Jaguar quarterback drops back and zips a pass intended for a tight end angling over the middle, a play that got them good yardage in their long drive, but Ricky steps in the way, intercepts the pass, sprints toward the sidelines, and cuts up-field. Protected by a phalanx of white-shirted blockers, he races the length of the field untouched for a Panther touchdown. With Donnie unable to kick the extra point, Charlie runs for the conversion, and we are up 7-0.

Ricky scores two more times before halftime – once on a punt return, another on a run around end from the offensive backfield. He intercepts another pass to stall a Bloomington drive just before halftime. The performance is the high point of Ricky's young life up to that time. Fifty years later, it remains so.

The Panthers go into halftime with a 27-0 lead. Things look pretty secure. I am already thinking about how I would open my story about the game -- Donnie's injury or Ricky's heroics. Although I am not privy to Coach Doggett's halftime talk, I imagine it is like dozens of others I had heard since my sophomore year: Blocking, tackling, fundamentals, execution, cursing, physical and verbal abuse, foaming, one cliché after another. I don't recall him ever saying anything good about any of us, at least not to our faces. For the time being, I am relieved to be in the bleachers and not in the field house. In all my playing days, I have never seen a marching band perform. Bloomington's band performs a routine that make the most complicated plays in our playbook -- with all their fakes, spins, and blocking schemes -- look simple by comparison. Afterwards, the Reitz 100 performs a spirited medley from *West Side Story* – "Somewhere," "I Feel Pretty," "Tonight." The drum major runs full speed ahead while leaning back so far his beefeater hat almost brushes the ground. After the bands play, a half–dozen convertibles carry the Homecoming court around the track. The girls smile gracious Homecoming court smiles and wave gracious Homecoming waves to the crowd on their way to the reviewing stand. Donnie McDowell, wearing a tan tuxedo with a white carnation in the lapel, hobbles out on crutches to escort Cindy Sullivan to the viewing stand, where they are crowned Homecoming Queen and King. The fact that Donnie is not wearing his grass-stained jersey with big number 66 on it does not bode well for the second half or for the rest of the season. Patty Nichols, who looks stunning in her light green chiffon gown and long, brown, curled hair, walks to the stand unescorted because her boyfriend Tony Reavis has not been dismissed from the locker room, where he is probably getting his ass chewed by Coach Doggett.

The second half opens with Ricky returning a kickoff 80 yards for another score. The rout is on, and we end up winning 46-0. (I say "we" tentatively since I am no longer a member of the team.)

THE DANCE

For the Homecoming dance, the school cafeteria has been magically transformed into a grand ballroom. Blue and gray streamers and balloons hang from the ceiling. All of the lunch tables have been folded up and stored away, except for one reserved for the Homecoming Court. Banners are draped throughout the hall, including one over the exit sign that reads: "Homecoming 1961: West Side Story."

"This place looks great," I remark.

"It should," says Martha. "I chaired the decorating committee."

"Is there any committee you're not on?"

"I don't think so."

In one corner of the room, the Continentals, wearing matching beige tuxedos and pompadour haircuts, sing and play the hits of the day – Roy Orbison, Gene Pitney, Elvis, Fats Domino, Sam Cooke, Del Shannon… Out on the dance floor, Ray Moon dances a slow tune with Jill Henderson. I am used to seeing Ray in a grubby football uniform. He is a surprisingly good dancer, and Jill looks hotter than I have ever seen her. I always thought she was kind of plain, even mousy, but she has pulled out all the stops on her hairdo, makeup, and dress. On this night, she is drop-dead gorgeous, and you can tell by the way they look at each other that they are deeply in love. Ray's rogue lock of hair that always falls across his forehead is for the time being combed back. Homecoming King and Queen Donnie McDowell and Cindy Sullivan rock back and forth on the dance floor. Donnie towers over her by at least a foot, even with Cindy wearing high heels. Clearly, Donnie's knees hurt him and he has a hard time moving to the music. When the song ends, and Chubby Checker's "Peppermint Twist" begins, he hobbles off the dance floor to the sidelines and his crutches.

"Too much torque on the old ligaments," he groans.

"How many games are you going to miss?" I ask.

"At least one. Maybe two."

"What do you think Coach would do if he knew you were dancing?"

"Probably make me limp up and down the chute. I think I've done all the dancing I'm going to do tonight."

"Tough luck, man."

"We could have used you out there tonight."

"I miss being there. I did a dumb thing."

"Come back on the team. Coach would probably let you."

"No, he wouldn't."

"You're right. But for what it's worth, I don't blame you. If I had it to do all over again, I'd stick with baseball. Baseball is fun. Football isn't."

Talking to someone who is no longer a teammate feels a little awkward at first, but I am already starting to think like a journalist. I scribble his comments in my notebook and mull over in my head how I might use them in my write-up of the game. (Of course, I would never use his comment about Coach Doggett. That could get him in trouble.)

As the night wears on, my classmates shuttle on and off the dance floor in the same manner players would shuttle on and off the football field, only the uniforms are different. For the girls it is flip hairdos, ponytails, and bubble cuts – lots of hairspray. For footwear it is high heels, pumps, or flats. Earlier in the week Principal Pierson, who is tall and gaunt to the point of being cadaverous, issued an edict that only flats be worn on the cafeteria floor, but that edict is largely ignored. And there are dresses, everything from colorful formals to culottes, a hybrid of skirt and pants worn by some of the more adventurous girls. For guys it is flat-tops and Butch-waxed pompadours, rented tuxedoes with neckties and cummerbunds, and spit-shined loafers. Before the night is over, neckties loosen, hair grows disheveled, and shoes are tossed in a pile by the dance floor. The band launches into Paul Anka's "Put Your Head on My Shoulder" when Martha taps me on mine.

"Do you want to dance?" she asks. "You've been ignoring me all night, you know."

"Sure," I say. "I'm not much of a dancer though."

"Follow my lead," she says.

I wrap my right arm around Martha's skinny waist, take her right hand in my left, and press my rented tux against her rented gown. Cued by the song, she buries her head into my shoulder. I close my eyes and breathe in her perfume, and we rock gently back and forth on the cafeteria floor, speechless and more or less in time to the music. The dance floor fills with other couples, some slow-dancing gracefully, others slogging clumsily, but for three and a half minutes, the whole universe consists of only Martha and me.

"Let's get some air," Martha whispers as the song comes to a close.

"Yeah. Air sounds good."

BUSTED

Located on the top of the hill, the Reitz High School parking lot is the make-out Mecca for generations of west side teens. My mom and dad used to make out there. My older brother may have been conceived there. From the summit, you can look far out over the Ohio River as it bends around the Evansville waterfront. At night the illuminated buildings of downtown Evansville, none of them over ten stories tall, cast their multi-colored reflections on the onyx surface of the river as it winds its way downstream toward its eventual rendezvous with the Mississippi.

"Looks like something Monet would paint," says Martha.

"Who?"

"Claude Monet. He was a French impressionist."

"I was thinking it looked like one of those paintings on black velvet you buy sometimes in the grocery store parking lot."

Martha rolls her eyes and slides next to me in the front seat of my brother's car. Still forbidden to drive the family car, I have borrowed the blue '59 Ford that belongs to my older brother Richard, and waxed it to a glossy sheen. Martha offered to drive, but I figured it was the guy's responsibility to provide transportation on a date as important as Homecoming. "Have fun and take care of her," Richard told me, winking as he tossed me the keys. By "her," he meant his car.

I turn on the radio and the heater and wrap my arm around Martha's bare shoulder. When the tubes warm up on the radio, the Lettermen are singing "The Way You Look Tonight." Henry Mancini's "Moon River" follows.

Perfect.

This is my first time on Makeout Mountain. I have listened for years to the folklore associated with the place, but I have never had a mountaintop experience of my own. I lean forward and kiss Martha. Our eyes close as our lips and tongues explore each other. When we disengage, she takes off her cat-eye glasses and pulls out the pins that hold her hair into a bun, and she unclips her earrings and tosses them into her cavernous purse. Her hair cascades down her white shoulders and she shakes her curls from side to side. Briefly I wonder if she has ever been here before, but I don't ask. I loosen my necktie, catch my breath, and we start kissing again. Before long we disappear into the front seat, and the river and the fuzzy dice that hang from Richard's rear view mirror are out of sight and out of mind. I move aside the spaghetti straps of her gown and fumble to unclasp her brassiere while she tosses aside my tie and starts unbuttoning my shirt. Then she works her way down to my trousers. Skillfully, she unhooks my belt and unzips my pants, all the while kissing me feverishly.

The sharp rap on the window stops us in our tracks. We bolt upright and hurriedly button those things that had been unbuttoned, clasp those things that had been unclasped, fasten those things that had been unfastened, and zip those things which had been unzipped. I roll down the window. It is Officer Henderson, Jill's dad. He shines a flashlight into the front seat.

"You kids can't do that here," he says. "You need to move along."

"Yes, sir."

"I didn't see you on the field tonight," he says. "Is that concussion still bothering you?"

"Yes, sir."

I roll up the window and look at Martha, who is refreshing her lipstick. My erection, which was as long and stiff as Officer Henderson's flashlight before the rap on the window, has diminished somewhat, but not much.

"What do you want to do?" I ask.

"Do you want to go back to the dance?"

"Not really."

"Me neither. Let's take a drive."

THE DELUGE

Raindrops bead up on the waxed hood of Richard's car as I lift my right hand from Martha's knee long enough to turn on the wipers, which slap across the windshield more or less in time to the wim-o-weh, wim-o-weh of "The Lion Sleeps Tonight" on the radio.

"So where do you want to go?" I ask.

"Burdette Park?"

"Sounds good."

The increased activity of the morality police on the hilltop in recent weeks has forced West Side teen-agers to seek new places to make out. One of those is

Burdette Park. After the swimming lake closes on Labor Day, few people have any reason to go there, unless they want to roller skate all day for seventy-five cents. At night Burdette is dark and quiet, and narrow lanes that twist through the park's wooded hills offer more privacy than the school parking lot, even if the view is less spectacular.

Lightning flashes and the rain falls harder. I turn up the wipers to keep pace with the rain on the windshield. Del Shannon sings "Runaway" on the radio: *I'm a walkin' in the rain. Tears are fallin' and I feel the pain...*

Perfect. When the lightning flashes, the radio crackles and pops. The rain falls so hard and so fast that I can hardly see the road.

"...wishin' you were here by me to end this misery and I wonder. I wa-wa-wa-wa wonder. Why. Wa-wa-wa-wa-why...."

At South Red Bank Road, Bayou Creek spills over its banks and submerges a good portion of the road. Because no one has erected a barricade, I don't fully comprehend what is going on until Richard's car churns through water up to the hubcaps. Then the car sputters and dies in midstream. I try to restart it but have no luck.

"What now?" asks Martha.

"I say we stay here and park like we planned," I suggest. "Nobody will bother us here."

"I'm serious, Gator. The water is rising. We've got to get out of here!!"

She is right, of course. The water is almost up to the door handle and seeping through the floorboard. I roll down the driver's window and climb out. Martha, who has stashed her high heels in her purse, climbs out the passenger window. Together we wade at least a half-mile through knee-deep water in a driving rainstorm until we get to a pay phone and call a tow truck. Martha's gown and my tux are wringing wet, too far gone to return to the rental store. Our clothes are plastered to our skin, and our perfect Homecoming hair lies plastered across our foreheads. It would be a great picture for the yearbook. For what it's worth, I don't get laid, and Richard's Ford never runs the same.

BULLSHIT TO BALONEY

The three weeks leading up to the last game of the season race by in a blur (as if the fifty years that followed didn't). On the political front, President Kennedy announces that he will send 16,000 "advisers" to South Vietnam to stem an increasing number of Communist raids from the north. In the entertainment world, insiders proclaim Groucho Marx the frontrunner in the scramble to replace Jack Paar as host of NBC's *Tonight Show.* A young comic named Johnny Carson is listed as a dark horse. Three westerns -- *Bonanza, Gunsmoke*, and *Wagon Train* -- are the three most watched television shows in America. On *Leave It to Beaver*, Beaver gets marooned in a giant coffee mug perched on top of a café, and *The Twilight Zone* airs an episode which poses the question "What would you do during a nuclear blast if your neighbor knocked on the door of your fallout shelter?" In sports, the Minnesota Vikings and the Dallas Cowboys win their first NFL games ever, beating the Chicago Bears and Pittsburgh Steelers respectively on the same Sunday afternoon.

Closer to home, a band of miscreants decorate my homeroom teacher's yard with toilet paper on Halloween night. Dressed in black, the raiders walk stealthily through the woods, straddle a fence, and creep along the perimeter of the property. From there, into the nearly leafless limbs of Mr. Madison's beloved oak trees, the raiding party launches roll after roll after roll of Charmin, their long paper trails streaming behind them as they sail through the chilly midnight air. Perhaps it is the thump of toilet paper on the ground, or maybe it is the crunch of shoes on fallen leaves that causes the family dog to bark and the living room lights to turn on. Everyone runs like hell back to the car, which is parked a good half-mile down the road. We think we get away with the caper, but Mr.

Madison calls everyone's parents the next day, and we spend the afternoon raking leaves and cleaning his yard.

There are also two high school football games.

We beat North's Huskies 26-0 on their field and keep the scoreless streak alive. The Huskies are 5-1 going into the game, and their quarterback, Mike Masterson, is the star pitcher on their state champion baseball team. But he has a trick knee, which pops out of joint three times during the game. (The only other injury of note was to one of the officials, who hurts his leg when he gets knocked down during the runback of the game-opening kickoff. But he scambles to his feet, sucks it up, and hobbles up and down the field for the duration of the game.) Masterson and his backup complete only four passes all night, and two of them land in the hands of Ricky Ferrell, who returns the last one sixty yards for a touchdown late in the fourth quarter that seals the victory and preserves the shutout.

The next game is against the third-ranked Memorial Tigers. They are 6-1, fresh from a gritty 14-7 win over Bob Griese and the previously unbeaten Rex Mundi Monarchs in a battle of parochial powerhouses. Rex Mundi is a brand new school, and because of scheduling conflicts, we do not play the Monarchs in 1961. (In the first meeting of the two schools a year later, the Panthers would win a brutal 7-0 defensive battle, in which a long touchdown run on a punt return by Griese was wiped out by a clipping penalty. Football fans have argued for years about who would have won had the '61 Monarchs played the '61 Panthers. We will never know, but I am pretty sure we would have whipped them.)

The newspapers hype the Reitz-Memorial game as if it were the high school Super Bowl. One sportswriter says that Memorial's line is bigger and stronger than the Panther line. Another claims that Memorial's fullback, Pete Miller, is better than Donnie McDowell. Fueling emotions further are the half-dozen big blue M's spray painted on the red brick exterior walls when we arrive at school on game day.

"The bastards!" says Hog.

Ray Moon is hopping mad: "Let's kill those god-damned mackerel snappers!"

"Easy, Ray," says Tony. "I'm Catholic, remember?"

Tony went to St. Agnes Elementary School in Howell, an autonomous part of town separated from the rest of Evansville by the L&N Railroad yards. He attended church at St. Agnes, and his uncle is the parish priest there. When it was time to enter high school, he opted for F.J. Reitz, the public school his father attended twenty-five years before.

"Sorry. I forgot," Ray apologizes.

The Panthers win 33-0. Charlie scores three times, all on short runs, and our backs pound repeatedly into

Memorial's defensive line like a battering ram softening the ramparts of a besieged medieval fortress. After enough thrusts, the Memorial line buckles and hemorrhages, and Kenny, Ricky, and Charlie are able to pick up yardage in three and four-yard chunks. The only long run of the evening is a reverse by Benny Cain, who races untouched into the end zone, escorted by his twin brother.

After the game I talk to Ray at Parkway.

"Was Memorial as good as they were cracked up to be?" I ask.

"They were tough enough, I guess, but all that crap about their line being better than ours is bullshit."

When I write my account of the game for the *Mirror,* I change "bullshit" to "baloney."

Undefeated, Untied, Unscored Upon

Entering the last week of the season, we are 8-0, ranked first in the state in both polls, and we have outscored our opponents 313-0. Our crosstown rivals, the Bosse Bulldogs are the only obstacle standing between the '61 Panthers and a place in the history books. I sit in the cheering section next to Martha. My reporter's notebook is in my jacket pocket, and a 35-millimeter camera hangs from my neck.

It is late in the fourth quarter, and we are way ahead, 55-0. Whether we will win or not is not the issue. The bigger issue is whether we could keep the Bulldogs out of our end zone. Five seconds remain on the clock and the Bulldogs, aided by a roughing the passer penalty and a successful fake punt, have driven to our five yard line on a cold, drizzly November night. Their quarterback, Steve Burris, calls time out and trots to the sidelines to consult his coach about whether to go for a field goal. The coach scratches his bald head a few seconds before vetoing the field goal and instructing his quarterback to go for six.

Ten-thousand fans wearing fur coats, gloves, and wool caps huddle under blankets, sip hot chocolate or other potables, and freeze their buns off on the cold concrete seats and aluminum bleachers, all anxious to see how history would play out. Our cheerleaders, sporting new angora earmuffs and hand-warmers, go through their familiar routines: "Push 'em back, push 'em back, way back!!!" "Two bits, four bits, six bits, a dollar. All for Panthers, stand up and holler!" Ray Moon and Tom Reavis dig in on the front line. Behind them Donnie McDowell, back in action after missing two games with a knee injury, crouches and waits, his blue eyes riveted on the quarterback, feet rocking back and forth, ready to pursue in any direction. The Cain twins guard the corners like rooks on a chessboard, and free safety Ricky Ferrell spits and draws a line with his cleats at the goal line.

Coach Doggett, wearing a trench coat and gray fedora, pops a couple of antacids and chomps rapidly. The Bulldogs, wearing their red and gray road uniforms, break from the huddle and line up at the five yard line. Steam escapes from everyone's nostrils as they take their positions along the line of scrimmage. Burris crouches behind center, barks the signal, takes the snap, and rolls right, pursued by Ray and Tony. With time running out, he spots an open receiver at the one yard line and heaves a wobbly pass toward the end zone as Tony and Ray smother him. The Bulldog receiver hauls in the pass at the one, but Ricky Ferrell drives him out of bounds as time expires, taking out the trombone section of the band in the process. I snap the picture. The final gun sounds, the band regroups and launches into the school song for the umpteenth time, and blue-gray confetti fills the chilly evening sky. Students, faculty, and fans form a conga line that wraps around Reitz Hill deep into the night. "Panthers win! Panthers win!" shouts Mr. Madison over the public address system. "Panthers win!"

Post-Season

Orbits and Obits

I sit in the journalism room on a rainy February afternoon, hunched over an old Olivetti typewriter, trying to find words to describe John Glenn's history-making orbit of the Earth. Mr. Larson's morning history class watched the event on a black and white television that had been rolled into his classroom. Walter Cronkite did the play-by-play. Watching and listening to history in the making brought a lump to my throat, and I was never more proud to be an American. Whether it is because of my lame typing skills – I made a C in Mrs. Dean's typing class as a junior – or because I can't find adequate words to describe such an earth-changing event, I am not making much headway on the page. I have typed the lead and part of the first paragraph when Coach Doggett strides into the room.

"Gates," he says.

"Yes, sir."

"We need someone to wrestle at 160 pounds. Can you do it?"

"Yes, sir."

"Gates, I noticed you up in the bleachers watching us practice. You miss competing, don't you?"

"Yes, sir. I do."

Guilt has been gnawing at me ever since I quit football, and I don't want quitting to be my high school legacy. I thought about going out for wrestling, but I figured I was still high on his shit list.

"I had been thinking about asking you back on the football team, but my pride got in the way," Coach confesses.

"I was going to ask you if I could come back, but I was afraid."

"I don't blame you, son. I would have been afraid too."

He assures me that he will give me a fresh start, and in exchange I agree to work hard, abide by his rules, and do all the bullshit he required of his wrestlers, which means innumerable trips up and down the chute, innumerable reps in the weight room, and interminable hours on the mat.

"So do you want to wrestle?"

"Yes, sir."

"Then report to the field house tomorrow afternoon after school."

Then he walks out the door, and that is the last time I see him alive. I learn about his death in next morning's

Courier. According to the article, Coach dropped his wife Louise off at the Baby Shoppe and then cruised around the block two or three times in search of a parking place. The heart attack struck after he parked the car. When he didn't come into the store, Louise went out into the rain to look for him. She heard the repeated blasting of the horn and followed the sound. She found her husband two blocks away, slumped over the steering wheel. The horn was blasting, the radio was on and the wipers were wiping. She ran into Woolworth's and called an ambulance, which arrived within minutes and carried Coach to Deaconess Hospital, where he was pronounced dead on arrival. The article appeared on the front page below the fold, underneath a wire service story about John Glenn's orbit.

The notion that Coach is dead doesn't seem possible. On the hill, he was immortal, bigger than life, and the notion that he could die seems more preposterous than putting a man on the moon, as President Kennedy had pledged to do by the end of the decade. But I suppose it was his time to move on. He achieved perfection, and what more is there to do once you achieve perfection?

Hog, holding back tears, tells me the next day that Coach dismissed wrestling practice early on the day he died. In my four years on the hilltop, I have never known him to dismiss practice early.

"I asked him if he felt okay, and he said he felt fine," says Hog, who labors just as hard to lose weight during wrestling season as he does to gain weight during football season. "But he looked tired."

I report for wrestling the next afternoon, and I gut the season out. I have an average year, winning about half my matches. Fifty years later, I am still wrestling.

GRADUATION

Our graduation ceremony takes place in The Bowl, where I have spent so many autumn days playing football. Martha Mattingly, our valedictorian, says something like "You are the future of America. Go forth and do great things...blah, blah, blah..." The band plays "Pomp and Circumstance" and I march across the stage to receive my diploma. It is hot as hell, and I am looking forward to the party afterwards at Hog's dad's river camp on Old Henderson Road, where there would be beer and liquor in abundance, including two cases of Sterling contributed by my brother Richard.

Colored Chinese lanterns are strung out across the yard, and the greatest hits of the summer of 1962 play over the loudspeaker. Everyone gets wasted. Ray climbs up to the center arch of the Old Henderson Railroad Bridge

and dives off to win a $10 bet. Martha Mattingly and
I make love on a squeaky bed in the cabin's back room,
whose knotty pine walls are decorated with trophy-sized
largemouth bass pulled from the river. It is our first time
in what will become our Summer of Love.

Lots of yearbooks are signed that night. I write
something corny in Martha's yearbook (of which she
was the editor) like "Thank you for a wonderful and
fun semester. Good luck at IU" or something equally
lame. I study the pictures and the captions beneath
them: **Martha Mattingly:** yearbook editor, Mirror staff,
Quill & Scroll, National Honor Society, National Junior
Honor Society, Pep Club, Homecoming Committee,
Prom Committee, Student Council; **Ray Moon**: Varsity
football, Projectionist Club; **Jill Henderson:** FBLA,
Library Assistant, Pep Club, FHA; **Donnie McDowell**:
Senior Class President, Varsity Football, Varsity Baseball,
Student Council, Homecoming King, National Honor
Society, National Junior Honor Society; **Kenny Cain:**
Varsity track, varsity football, History Club, NJHS;
Benny Cain: Varsity track, varsity football, History Club,
Thespians, NJHS; **Tony Reavis:** Senior Class Treasurer,
Varsity Football, Varsity Basketball, Concert Choir,
Student Council, National Honor Society, National
Junior Honor Society, National Forensic League; **Cindy
Sullivan**: Varsity Cheerleader, Homecoming Queen,

NHS, NJHS, Panther Performers, Pep Club, Student Council; **Patty Nichols**: Homecoming Court, Student Council, FHA, FBLA, NHS, NJHS, Prom Committee; **Richard Johnson:** Varsity Football, Varsity Wrestling, Varsity Baseball, Varsity Golf; **Charlie Cassidy**: Varsity Football, Varsity Basketball, Varsity Baseball, Varsity Track, NHS, Student Council. Then there is me: **Russell Gates**: Quill & Scroll, Varsity Wrestling, Varsity Baseball, Reserve Football. Not pictured is Ricky Ferrell.

I look at the photos: the one where Charlie set a school high jump record at the city track meet after I drove him there from the baseball field, where he just finished a complete game shutout. He changed from his baseball uniform and cleats into his track silks and spikes in the back seat of my dad's car en route to the stadium. And of course there's the one I took at the tail end of the Bosse game where Ricky knocks a Bosse receiver out of bounds on the one-yard line as time expires. There are lots of other black and white pictures too – club pictures, prom pictures, Homecoming pictures, sports photos, faculty photos.

(Fast forward fifty years: Sometimes I wish I still had my old high school yearbook, but my mother accidentally gave it away, along with several thousand baseball cards I had been collecting since the fourth grade, when she donated my old desk to Goodwill while I was in Vietnam. They would be worth a fortune today. Oh well.)

DIASPORA

After graduation, we spend the summer pretty much doing what we have always done – hang out at Parkway, the drive-in, and Burdette Park, which now boasts a brand new Olympic-size pool to take the place of the old salt pond. But come mid-August, we all go our separate ways. Donnie accepts a scholarship to the University of Illinois, where he will play linebacker alongside Dick Butkus for two years, go to the Rose Bowl, and get drafted by the Minnesota Vikings. Tony Reavis enrolls in the Air Force Academy, where he would learn how to fly jets and drop bombs. Trish and Cindy, their steady girlfriends, remain in Evansville. They would later marry their sweethearts. Benny and Kenny Cain, who ran leadoff and anchor legs of the Panthers' record-setting mile relay team during the spring, accept track scholarships to Southern Illinois University, where they would run on the nation's fastest collegiate mile relay. Hog also goes to Southern, where he would be the Salukis' starting center for three years. Charlie Cassidy goes to Vanderbilt, where would play in the defensive backfield and would be praised by Alabama's Bear Bryant as the hardest hitter in the Southeastern Conference. Ricky takes a job at the local bottle cap factory and hustles pool on the side. Ray Moon marries Jill Henderson and gets a job on the loading dock at the Mead

Johnson plant at the foot of the hill. Having no scholarship offers, average grades, and no money, I go to work there too. It feels funny not to be reporting to football practice.

Martha Mattingly goes off to school at Indiana University to study journalism. Then she fades out of my life, the way a carhop skates away after she serves you. I get four letters from her during that first semester she is at Bloomington: the first one, which is dowsed in perfume, to say how much she misses me; the second to tell me she is pregnant; the third a few weeks later to tell me she lost the baby; and the fourth to inform me that she is seeing a rich, well-connected fraternity man. I offer to marry her after her second letter, but her third and fourth letters make that offer unnecessary.

I respond the way I always respond to adversity: I get drunk.

Do I miss her? Hell yes! She was fun. Did I love her? In my clumsy 17-year-old way, I suppose so. I loved her the best way I knew how. No regrets. For what it's worth, I save her letters. The first one still smells of perfume. But I've long since moved on, sort of, and so has she.

We've Got to Get Out of this Place

Ray and I sit on a pile of skids on the loading dock, shooting the shit and watching the sun set between the twin smokestacks, like we do almost every workday afternoon. Ray munches on a tuna fish sandwich Jill prepared for him. I chain-smoke Marlboro reds.

"I just don't understand why you smoke that shit," Ray says.

"Yeah? Well I don't understand why you don't."

"Your lungs are going to look like the inside of that smokestack one of these days."

"Something is going to get us eventually. Might as well be cigarettes."

I exhale, stub out my cigarette, and flick the butt out into the parking lot.

"I got my draft notice yesterday," I say matter-of-factly.

"Bastard. I envy you."

"What's to envy? I'm probably on the fast track to Vietnam. That's turning into a pretty nasty little war, from everything I'm hearing."

"I'd give anything to go – anything to get out of this shit hole. I tried to enlist in the Army twice, but they wouldn't take me. They said I weighed too much for my height. Twice I took the test to join the city fire department, but they didn't want me either. Politics, you know. So here I am."

"That sucks. So, what are you going to do? Sit on the dock of the loading bay and watch the time slip away?"

"Now you sound like Jill."

"I was going for Otis Redding. Sorry, man. Just asking."

"I've been thinking about the Marine Corps. They've been seeing a lot of action around Da Nang lately. Maybe I can get in on it. If that doesn't pan out, I guess I'll work here on the docks until I die."

"Another day that will live in Enfamil," I say, trying to parody Franklin Roosevelt.

"Count yourself lucky that you're staying home, Ray. Vietnam is a real shithole, from what I hear."

"How much worse can it be than Evansville in August?"

"You've got a point."

"I want to fight for my country like my dad did and like his dad did."

"You still want to be Big Bad John, don't you?"

"Somebody's got to prop up the dominoes, Gator."

"Hey Ray, have you heard whether the team is going to be any good this year?"

"Not as good as us. Nobody will ever be as good as us. From what I hear, they're running out of a T-formation now, and their star halfback is a colored kid."

"The times, they are a changin'."

Bus Station

I am down at Fort Benning, Georgia, learning to fly helicopters when I learn that my father has died. The

Army grants me a pass to attend the funeral. I stand at the Greyhound Station in Indianapolis buying a ticket to Evansville when I unexpectedly run into Ray.

"Gator, what the hell are you doing up here?" hollers Ray.

"Catching a bus to Evansville. What about you?"

"Me too. I just joined the Marine Corps. Got tired of waiting on the fire department."

"Looks like you're going to be a firefighter after all."

"What brings you to back to Indiana?"

"Dad died. Heart attack."

"Sorry, man."

We board the bus and shoot the shit all the way back to Evansville. It's about a five-hour bus trip, seeing as the bus stops at every two-bit town along the way. We talk a little about Vietnam, a little about football, and a little about my father, but mostly we joke around like we used to when we were riding the team bus. When we tire of talking, we play dominoes for a while, and when we run out of things to talk about, we stare out the window. Ray falls asleep.

Lots of things roll through my mind as I watch a pink and purple sunset beyond the cornfields of central Indiana. The same sun is rising about now over a rice paddy in Southeast Asia, where a man in a cone-shaped hat walks behind his water buffalo. And I think about Dad. What do you say about a man you have known since day one? Sure, we fought bitterly all through my high school years. But he taught me how to hunt and fish. And he built a tree house for Richard and me when we were kids. That tree house was the envy of all the neighborhood kids. It had a trap door, a balcony, a deck on the roof, and a guard tower where we could see for miles in all directions. We had a no-girls rule, but we waived it after a while, mostly at Richard's urgings. Mom found Dad dead in his hammock. He looked like he was sleeping. He just didn't wake up. I loved him but I never told him. I try to hold back tears, but I can't.

"It's OK, man," says Ray, who has awakened somewhere down the line. "I envy you, Gator. I barely knew my dad."

We wheeze into the bus station around midnight, where Jill waits in her car the way she used to do every afternoon after every football practice.

After they embrace, she hands him a letter from the Evansville Fire Department. He tears it open and sighs. He learns he has been accepted into the firefighter training program. It's the last time I see him alive.

JULY 1972

It is late in July 1972 when I learn that the B-52 Tony Reavis is piloting goes down somewhere over the jungles of Thailand, killing all on board. The Air Force tells Tony's family that it is a weather-related incident. They say lightning struck the plane, causing all the instruments to go dead.

Tony is one of the last casualties of the war. The ground fighting has ceased, but President Nixon is still authorizing bombing raids to pursue the enemy into their sanctuaries across the border in Cambodia and to force the North Vietnamese into signing a peace agreement. America has had enough of Vietnam and most folks want us to get the hell out in the most expedient way possible. Tony is completing his second tour. In his first tour, he flew C-130 troop and equipment transport planes. In his second, he drops bombs.

I am one of the pallbearers at his funeral, along with Donnie McDowell, Charlie, Hog, and Benny Cain. Donnie has just moved to Atlanta to play for the Falcons. Charlie works as an accountant somewhere near Chicago. Benny lives with his mother in the house where he grew up on the hill. Kenny isn't present.

It is a hot day in August when Tony's remains are laid to rest, way too hot for sport coats and neck ties. Birds chirp and the scent of freshly cut grass wafts across the cemetery grounds. Patty, dressed in black, sits in a folding chair. Tears cause her mascara to run. Tony's mom, dad, siblings, and two young children sit beside her. Others gathered under the canopy include numerous classmates, relatives, comrades in arms, and friends. Father Bob, Tony's uncle, says a few words of comfort, and then an Air Force colonel hands a flag folded into a triangle to Tony's mother.

"From a grateful nation," the colonel says.

Then the casket, which has been closed all during visitation at the funeral home, is lowered into the ground. A team of riflemen fire a 21-gun salute, and then a trio of jets flies in formation overhead, their long white vapor trails superimposed against a cloudless blue sky.

Benny

After the service, Benny Cain and I drive to the Hilltop Inn to get drunk. He's put on about twenty pounds since high school, but he still looks like he can run a quarter mile under fifty seconds.

"What are you doing these days, Gator?" he asks.

"I'm a stockbroker."

"Really?"

"No, not really. I'm not doing much of anything really. I drink beer. I shoot pool. I'm still trying to figure out what I want to do when I grow up."

"Me too."

I can't look at Benny without thinking of Kenny, so I pop the question: "Where's Kenny?"

"Your guess is as good as mine, Gator."

"So what happened? You guys used to be so close."

"We got into a fight during our senior year at SIU. When we were juniors at SIU we ran on the top college mile relay team in the country. Nobody beat us all year. Kenny ran the first leg. I ran anchor, just like high school. But during our senior year, Kenny started skipping classes and drinking heavily – bourbon, at least a fifth a day. His grades dropped, and he caught hepatitis that made him really, really sick. I was worried about him so I confronted him one day in front of our dormitory. He had been drinking all day. He was thin, and his complexion was yellow."

"Kenny, man you look like shit. You'd better get your act together. Track season starts in a few weeks!"

"Fuck track!" I never wanted to run track. I never even liked track if you want to know the truth. I wanted to go to Butler and play football, but for some damn reason I followed you here."

"You've got to stop drinking, man. You're going to kill yourself."

"Fuck you! If I want to kill myself, that's my business. I'm sick and tired of always doing what you do. Shit, man. We've done the same stuff for twenty years. We shared the same car – even dressed the same. I hate track and I hate you."

"Come on Kenny. You're drunk! Let's go inside."

"I moved toward him, but he swung at me. I dodged the blow, but I landed awkwardly on the curb and broke my ankle. That ended my track career and it pretty much marked the point where Kenny and I parted company. Neither of us ran track that spring. I hung around and graduated, but Kenny dropped out of school. Last I heard, he and Hog joined the Army. I guess they figured if they enlisted on the buddy plan, they wouldn't get shipped to Nam. They could be in the Swiss Alps or they could be in Fort Knox. I really don't know."

Forty Years Later...

I stand in the driveway of Mom's house, the same brownstone bungalow I grew up in, on the south side of Reitz hill, loading furniture into the back of my pickup truck -- the old kitchen table where I ate thousands of meals, the old console TV from our living room, the recliner from which I used to watch that television, and some other odds and ends. Benny stops by on his mountain bike. Wearing gray sweat clothes and a Cardinals baseball cap, he looks about 100 pounds heavier than his playing days. It has to be Benny because I got word a few years ago that Kenny had died.

"What's up, Gator?"

"Not much, man. Just loading some stuff from the old house. Mom died a few weeks back, and the house will be up for sale soon."

"I'm sorry, man. I hadn't heard."

"That's OK. So where are you these days?"

"Still on the hill."

"What are you doing?"

"I keep busy. I ride my bike. I'm trying to get skinny again. And I take care of Mom. She's 93 years old now."

"Tell her howdy for me, will you?"

"I will, but I doubt she will remember who you are."

"If you don't mind my asking, what happened to Kenny?"

"Long story."

"I've got time."

"Remember when I told you that he had a bout of hepatitis back in college?"

"Yeah."

"After he got out of the Army, Kenny went to work in Louisville as an airplane mechanic, and he was always around toxic chemicals. The chemicals, we think, gave him cancer, and the hepatitis he had back in college left his immune system too weak to fight it. He died in 1995. I miss him, Gator. I really do," says Benny, choking back tears. "It's hard to explain, but it's like a piece of me is missing."

"I'm sorry, man. I understand."

It is all I can think of to say. I don't mean to tear open any more emotional scabs, so I change the subject. Men are good at that.

"Are you going to the 50-year reunion?" I ask.

"Nah," Benny says. "I haven't given high school a thought, or football for that matter, since I graduated. I think it's best to leave all that in the past. What about you?"

"Not sure. I haven't been to any reunions yet. I missed the first one because of Vietnam and the rest of them because I was too embarrassed to show up. I didn't want to show up unless I was successful, you know? Plum job, trophy wife, all that. Never happened. But part of me wants to go to this one. It might be my last chance to see some folks before they pass on. Hell, Benny, I'm almost 70 years old. Do you believe that? How the hell did that happen?"

"One day at a time."

"Our parents are dying, man. I'm dying. We're all dying."

Before long, I start sobbing. Benny and I hug awkwardly, the way aging jocks do. Then he hops back on his bike and resumes pedaling up the hill.

"Later, Gator!" he hollers.

Hardly anyone has called me 'Gator' since high school.

NOVEMBER 2011

I cough a cloud of blue-gray smoke into the cold, black November night. It's an annoying, hacking cough I've had for a few years, no doubt the consequence of fifty years of smoking. The night is perfect football weather. I attended the school's Homecoming game last night, but I didn't get to walk out on the field at halftime to be honored as a member of the '61 Panthers, who after fifty years, are still the only team in Indiana high school history to complete an entire season without yielding a point.

I almost don't come to my 50-year reunion. My first impulse is to crumple up the invitation and toss it in the trash can like I had done all the others. But my therapist convinces me to come. She says it will be good to confront my old ghosts. My AA sponsor advises me to stay home and leave the ghosts and the cash bar alone. Truth be told, I don't give a shit. All I want to do is make peace with my past and see some of my old classmates before they check out. And maybe part of me wants want to get laid. Damn, it's been a long, long time. The magic blue pills are in the inside jacket pocket, just in case. The night air is chilly and the tree line off in the distance gives me the creeps. I take a deep breath, steel my spine, and make a resolution: I'm going in.

With its parquet floor and blue and gray balloons and streamers, the Exhibition Hall reminds me of Homecoming night back in 1961. (Where does one get gray balloons anyway?) The music is the same too – Sam Cooke, Dion and the Belmonts, the Shirelles – except the tunes are orchestrated by a hired disc jockey instead of a live band. Connie Francis croons *"Where the boys are, someone waits for me...."* I think about Jill Henderson.

A slender woman with a mane of silver-gray hair sits at the registration table. Even without her name tag, I recognize Patty Reavis. She was Patty Nichols in high school. Patty had, and still has, the most beautiful eyebrows – full, dark, and brown. Back in high school, she looked like a teen-aged Jackie Kennedy. She favors Emmylou Harris now. I sign the registration book and autograph my mug shot in the school yearbook.

"Russell Gates!" Patty says. "How've you been?"

"Not bad, considering."

"Considering what?"

"Considering I'm a 68-year-old man who's been through a war and three wives," I joke. "What are you doing these days?"

"Mostly enjoying my grandchildren. What about you? Do you have grandkids?"

"Yeah, but I don't know them."

"So what are you doing these days?"

"Retired," I say, too embarrassed to say I haven't held a steady job in years. "Trying to write."

"You were always good at that. What are you writing?"

"I said I was *trying* to write. Mostly I just drink coffee and stare at a blank screen. I've got a story but I don't know how to tell it -- a memoir of a fucked up life. Just trying to make sense of some things, you know?"

I realize too late that I said "fucked up" when "messed up" or "squandered" might have been a better rhetorical choice, given my audience and my situation. Tact has never been my strong suit.

"Pardon my language," I stammer.

"Don't worry about it," she says, smiling a broad, beautiful smile. The big, sparkly diamond on the ring finger of her left hand shouts: "I've long since remarried. Don't even think about hitting on me."

I cough into my sleeve.

"Nasty cough you've got there," she comments. "Maybe you ought to see a doctor."

"Maybe I will."

"Good seeing you," she says. "Let's get together sometime."

"Yes, let's."

I'm pretty sure we never will.

A collage of newspaper clippings glued onto a pair of poster boards next to the cash bar catches my eye. The headline arching over the display proclaims: "1961 Reitz Panthers: Undefeated, Untied, Unscored Upon." Pictured beneath are mug shots of the '61 Panthers, celebrating in the locker room after their last game of the season.

"What are doing, Gator? Trying to find your picture? You won't find it."

I turn. It's Hog Johnson. In high school, he always wanted to gain weight. Clearly, over time, he has figured that out. What hair he has left is gray and tied into a little rat-tail that disappears under the collar of his burgundy shirt. He loosens his Elvis necktie – the gyrating, pre-Hollywood Elvis, not the bloated Elvis parody of the '70s.

"Hog! How the hell are you?"

"Not bad for an old man."

"Still in food service?"

"Nope. Retired from that a few years ago," he says and hands me a business card.

It says "Richard Johnson Motorcycle Ministries." Beneath that, in red ink and italics is Matthew 25:36: *"I was naked and you clothed me; I was sick and you visited me; I was in prison and you came to me."* I put the card in my wallet.

"So you ride a bike?"

"Oh yeah. Harley."

"I've got a Harley too -- rode it here tonight."

"Cool! Let's go riding one of these days."

"You're on, man."

"Hey, can I buy you a drink?" he offers.

"Sure. I'll have a Coke."

"No rum? No bourbon? That's not the Gator I remember."

"You're buying? That's not the Hog I remember."

"Good for you. So what were you in such deep thought about, Gator?"

"I was having a flashback. Thinking about Ray..."

"Yeah. I think about him every now and then too. Just the other night I was thinking about that night at Parkway when he blew his hand up with a cherry bomb."

"I remember that."

"A lot of us are gone, Gator. Ray, Tony, Kenny...."

"Any idea what happened to Ricky Ferrell?"

"I saw him hustling pool down at the Sportsman about ten years ago, but that's the last I saw of him. My best guess is he's either dead or in jail."

The conversation sputters and stalls for a few seconds, and we observe an awkward moment of silence in remembrance of our fallen comrades. Hog picks it up again.

"So what have you been doing for fifty years?"

"Not much. Mostly under-achieving."

"Still?"

Hog brings me a Coke in a clear plastic cup and a beer for himself.

"How is your mom these days?" he says.

"Mom died a few months back. I went over to check on her one morning and found her dead, sitting on the toilet. Heart attack."

"Sorry to hear that. She was a great lady. She made the best peanut butter and jelly sandwiches on the west side."

I look around. A mirrored disco ball over the dance floor casts dots of light around the room. A panic attack washes over me like a tsunami. Suddenly I am back in the jungle. I've got to get away from the noise, and the people, and the flashing lights.

"Excuse me, Hog. I've got to use the bathroom."

"You've got that problem too?" he says.

I lean against the urinal, eyes closed, straining like a rusty, creaky oil well to siphon up what little liquid has pooled beneath the surface. Hog may have been joking, but he was on target. I have to pee way too often, especially at night, and when I go, I have to prime the pump for a few minutes, and when it comes, it erupts in a weak trickle. When I was young, I used to gush for minutes at a time. I haven't gushed in years.

"Will You Still Love Me Tomorrow?" by the Shirelles plays over the bathroom loudspeakers. Not that long ago, I weighed 150 pounds, and I had dark, close-cropped hair. Going into my senior year, I was first on the depth charts at tailback. I think back to a sunny afternoon, right before the season started, when we were scrimmaging on the practice field. In my head, I replay that long run: *Hog centers the ball to Charlie, who spins and hands off to me. I shoot toward tackle, veer to the right, find a crack of daylight, sprint down the sidelines, pick up a block by Kenny Cain, or maybe it's Benny, cut back to the inside, break a tackle, and coast into the end zone...*

"Gator?"

I open my eyes. Donnie McDowell gushes beside me. In high school he stood 6-3 and weighed around 200 pounds, but I remember him as much bigger. (Objects in the rear-view mirror are bigger than they actually are, I guess.) Since then, he's added fifty pounds of bulk, all muscle. He looks like he could still play linebacker, even though he retired from the NFL back in the '70s. Remarkably, Donnie's hair is still blond.

"Hey, Donnie. How's it going?"

"Can't complain. What about you?"

"I could but I won't. Still in Atlanta?"

"Still in Atlanta. Still with Cindy. Got a bunch of kids and grandkids."

"All blond?"

"Most of them."

"Is there life after football? What are you doing these days?"

"I'm in pharmaceutical sales."

"I used to do that. Almost did jail time for it."

"Ha! Same old Gator. Are you still married to – what's her name?"

"Nah, what's her name left years ago."

"Sorry. What happened?"

"Mostly I drank too much and couldn't keep my pecker in my pants."

"Seeing anybody?"

"Nope. Unemployed and unaffiliated."

"Maybe you'll get lucky tonight."

"Maybe." But I know the odds of meeting a single 68-year-old woman who is seeking a balding sixty-eight-year-old wannabe writer are pretty long.

Don zips up and limps to the lavatory.

"So how are the knees these days?" I ask.

"They're holding up. They're in as good a shape as they can be considering they've been through a dozen operations. They're pretty banged up, but they're still my original knees. Thank God for golf carts. Cindy's the one who's had replacement surgery. I guess cheerleading can be hard on the knees too."

I shake the last droplets into the urinal, put my pecker in my pants, and zip up. Urinal conversations are never very long or very deep or very comfortable.

"Nice talking to you," I say.

"Yeah, you too. Maybe we can get together and play golf or go turkey hunting over Thanksgiving."

"Yeah, maybe. Give me a call."

As Donnie leaves the bathroom, Ray Charles' "Hit the Road Jack" leaks in for a few seconds, and I flash back to our road trip to New Albany – the pre-game talk, Hog tossing his cookies in the huddle, the stop at the diner in Dale, dining on forbidden fruit in the back of the bus…

I walk to the sink, lather my hands, and stare in the mirror. *What the fuck happened to me? Where did my hair go? Where did these crows' feet come from? Since when did I start wearing bifocals?* For a split second, the seventeen-year-old Russell Gates looks back at me. He's slender, maybe 150 pounds, and he's confident, bordering on cocky. His dark hair is combed and expertly parted – just like the picture in the yearbook. I splash some cold water on my face and I morph back to my old self. I need a cigarette.

JILL

I stub out my Camel in a planter outside the Exhibition Hall, fumble for another cigarette, cup my hands, and try to light it with a cheap-ass convenience store lighter. My hands shake and my fingers sting. A light fog settles in. The dark tree line across the field reminds me of An Hoa on nights when I would stand guard on the perimeter, usually high on some killer Vietnamese weed, and stare off into a gray line of trees a half mile away. Those trees look innocent enough, but every now and then you can hear the staccato of an AK-47 or the thunder from a mortar that would sometimes lob shells within the base, and sometimes a sniper's bullet finds its mark on a stoned-out soldier whose mind strays from the here and now. Tree line at night gives me the creeps. Don't even ask me about the Fourth of July.

"How's it going, Gator?" says a voice from the fog.

I turn nervously, braced for combat.

"Easy, soldier," says Jill Henderson Moon.

"Jill!"

"What are you doing?'

"Smoking a cigarette. Flashing back."

"Can I have a cigarette?"

"Sure."

"Ray would have a fit if he knew I smoked. He hated cigarettes."

"Yes, he did."

I offer her a cigarette and light it.

"What have you been up to?" I ask. It is easily the most frequently asked question of the evening.

"Just retired from the public library. Been there forty-five years." She looks like a librarian – skinny, almost frail, gray hair, granny glasses resting on the bridge of her nose.

"Are you married, Gator?" she asks.

I exhale.

"Everyone seems to want to know that tonight. But no, I'm not -- not at the moment anyway."

"Me neither."

"Did you ever remarry?"

"No, never did. Ray was the love of my life. He was the only one."

"He would have enjoyed being here tonight, I think. He really liked to be around his friends."

"I remember the day I learned Ray had been killed like it was yesterday," she says. "I was shelving books at the library when two Marines in their dress blues approached me."

"Jill Henderson Moon?" says one soldier

"Yes, sir. How may I help you?"

"Are you the wife of Pfc. Douglas Ray Moon?"

"Yes. Is he all right?"

"Ma'am, we're sorry to report that your husband has been killed in a firefight in Quang Tri Province."

"I dropped my stack of books and just started weeping right there in general collections. Just one day before, I received a letter from Ray. He was real upbeat and he felt like he was doing some good in Vietnam. He said that me missed me and couldn't wait to get home and have a cold beer and a hot shower. He said the showers were cold and the beer was warm where he was."

"That's Vietnam, all right."

"The Marines stayed with me all through the week and through the funeral services. They acted like pit bulls, keeping people away from me, people I didn't want to talk to. They were very nice and very courteous, but as soon as the service was over, they were gone. The angels of death went back to wherever they came from, and I found myself alone. I'm still alone."

"I'm sorry," I say.

"Let's go inside," she says. "It's cold out here."

"I'll be in as soon as I finish my cigarette."

She does not know that I am the one who picked up Ray's body from the battlefield. Nobody knows that except me.

Shit. All Ray wanted to do was hold the line against communism the way he held the line for the '61 Reitz Panthers. He learned the hard way that no lines existed in Vietnam. There were no rules of engagement. It was a home game for Charlie. He knew and loved his homeland and fought fiercely for it. He fought the Chinese, the Japanese, and the French before he got around to fighting us. He knew how to fight, and he had a deep bench. No matter how many dinks we killed, they always found more to replace them. Fighting them was like fighting the Hydra: you chop off one head and two grow back. Charlie fought on his turf and on his terms. He fought when he wanted, where he wanted, and he disappeared like a fucking ghost, melted into the jungle, and blended into the general population when he didn't want to fight. Beating Charlie would have simple if he just had the etiquette to line up opposite us like a football scrimmage on a flat field with rules and boundaries, but Charlie didn't play that way. The worst part is that no one knew the score. The generals kept telling us we were winning, but I got to where I didn't believe them.

I mash out my cigarette and go back inside.

MARTHA

A woman half my age wipes the bar top. She has a rose tattoo on her hand and a pierced nose. She wears big hoop earrings and dark eye makeup. The name tag on her bar apron says "Tiffany." If I were twenty years younger, I would probably hit on her. I may hit on her anyway. A football game is on the big-screen television behind her.

"Who's playing?" I ask.

"Who knows?" she shrugs. "Can I get you something?"

"Rum and Coke, please, with a piece of lime."

"Cuba libre coming up. Four dollars."

The drink will be the first I've had this century. I feel anxious and out of place. A good stiff drink might calm my nerves and loosen me up socially. I hand her a five-dollar bill and she takes it upon herself to keep the change. While I wait for my drink, I check my cell phone for messages. Nothing new. Just a reminder that tonight is my 50-year high school reunion and another informing me that my annual prostate examination is next week. I haven't studied. I hope I pass.

"Howdy, stranger."

I swivel on my bar stool and pocket my phone. Martha Mattingly sits on the adjacent stool. Gone are the cat-eye glasses and the fluffed up hair. Her hair is dark with one gray streak running through it. She wears a black dress, black stockings, and black high heels. She carries a black purse.

"Martha! How are you?"

"Not bad for an old woman. You?"

"Not bad for an old man. You look wonderful."

"Bullshit. I look like a whore and you know it."

"That's not necessarily a bad thing."

"What's new?"

"Just dicking around. Riding my motorcycle. Trying to write."

"You were always good at that."

"Thanks. I try to write a little bit every day. Keeps me off the streets."

"I meant dicking around."

"Ha ha. Good one. What about you? Are you married?"

"No."

"Seeing someone?"

"Same old Gator, aren't you?"

"Hey, I'm just curious. I haven't seen you for almost fifty years – just trying to catch up."

"Yes. I'm seeing someone."

"Is he here tonight?"

"Why do you assume it's a he?"

I pause to process her comment.

"You're kidding, right?"

She smiles one of those ambiguous Mona Lisa smiles but says nothing.

"What about you, Gator? Are you married?" she asks.

"Divorced. Three times. I can't seem to get it right."

"Do you want to dance?"

"Sure."

She takes my hand and leads me to the dance floor just as Tiffany lays my Cuba libre on the bar top. The mirrored ballroom globe casts dots of light around the dance floor as the disc jockey spins a short medley by

Little Anthony and the Imperials. "I Think I'm Going out of My Head" fades and segues into the opening line of "Tears on My Pillow": *"You don't remember me, but I remember you..."*

Don and Cindy McDowell slow dance just like they did fifty years ago at Homecoming. He still towers over her. How people can stay together for fifty years is a mystery to me. But there they are: the captain of the football team and the Homecoming Queen, still together, living proof that happily ever after is not just a myth. I press Martha close enough to look into her brown eyes, eyes I have not gazed into for fifty years. I still suck at dancing, but she tolerates me. I press against her breasts, which seem smaller than those I used to gawk at from my lifeguard perch at Burdette Park.

"Mastectomy," she says, reading my mind. "About ten years ago."

"Sorry," I mumble.

"It's okay."

I close my eyes, breathe in Martha's perfume – patchouli, I think -- and flash back to Homecoming night, 1961.

"The Way You Look Tonight" is playing. I tell Martha that I like her perfume. Jill dances with Ray, who looks out of character in his rented tuxedo. The rogue lock of hair falls over his forehead. They dance close together, her head resting on his shoulder...

The soft, romantic music shifts gears, and "The Twist" by Chubby Checker pours out of the speakers. Most of the slow dancers exit the dance floor. Don and Cindy try to twist, but the Don's knees are too tender, so they sit down.

"Feel like twisting?" I ask.

"Why not? Let's do it. You only live once, right?"

So we twist until we are too exhausted to dance any more.

"Feel like getting some air?" I say, too tired to twist any more.

Martha smiles.

"Some old Gator," she says.

"I just want some fresh air and a cigarette. I swear."

"Is that really what you want?"

"Last call for fresh air. Are you sure?"

"Maybe later, Gator. It was good seeing you."

Martha and I leave the dance floor. She heads to the hors d'oeuvres table, and I head back to the bar. I sip my Cuba libre and swish it around in my palate, savoring the intermingled tastes of the dark rum, the Coke, and the lime. Then I spit it all into a plastic potted plant, just the way I used spit out the forbidden water during football practice.

Where the Boys Are

I seat myself at a table where Hog and Donnie talk politics over beer. Cindy sits next to Donnie. She is still strikingly beautiful and still blond. Hog sits next to a woman who exposes way more cleavage than a woman her age ought to. I assume she is his wife.

"Our parents were tougher than we are. They lived through a Depression. They had to be tough," Hog blusters. He is on his fourth or fifth beer. "At the game last night, our boys could have won, but they just gave up in the fourth quarter. Just when they needed to toughen up, they caved in. Athletes today all think they're entitled to something. They've bought into this entitlement mentality that prevails today."

"The programs that saved America were entitlement programs," I interject. "If it weren't for the New Deal, many of our parents would not have made it. I thank God for entitlement."

Hog takes the bait.

"But look. Today we've got schools without prayer, homosexuals teaching our kids, teenage girls getting abortions..."

"A black man in the White House?"

"I never said that," says Hog. "But you've got to admit, back in our day we didn't have all the problems we have today. We ought to return to some of those values."

"Back when a woman's place was in the kitchen, a queer's place was in the closet, and a nigger's place was on his side of town?"

"Make fun if you like," interjects Hog. "But look at some of the things the Supreme Court has allowed over the years. James 3:4 says *"Look also at the ships: although they are so large, they are turned by a very small rudder."* That small rudder, in my opinion, is our Supreme Court. Truth is, we don't have the same leadership today as we did when we were growing up. Back then we had leaders we could trust and respect and look up to. Eisenhower was a leader. Coach Doggett was a leader."

That's all I need to hear.

"I'm not going to get into a Bible quoting match, Hog, because you'll win," I say. "And, true, maybe there are some time-tested values we ought to revisit, but I don't ever want to return to a time when abuse was a common and accepted practice. You're entitled to your opinion about Coach. But in my opinion, he was a mean old man."

"A winner never quits. A quitter never wins. And you're a quitter, Gates," shouts Hog. "You're a quitter and you're a loser. You were then, and you are now."

"The only thing I'm going to lose is my temper."

"We've become a nation of quitters," Hog continues. "If we hadn't quit in Vietnam, we'd have won. But we quit when things got tough. Makes me want to puke."

"Did you go to Vietnam?"

"No..."

"Well I did. While you were hiding out in college, getting shitfaced at fraternity parties, snapping footballs and looking at the world between your legs, I was off in the jungle. So don't talk to me about Vietnam, you hypocrite. And if you call any of us who did serve there quitters, I'll strangle you with my bare hands. And don't think I can't do it. I've been trained to do it."

"I think maybe you'd better leave," says Donnie, rising from the table, dinner napkin still tucked into his trousers.

"Yeah, maybe so."

I should know better than to get into political arguments, especially with people who have been drinking, and I ought to know better than to ridicule values others hold dear. Hell, one man's sacred cow is another man's hamburger.

"See you guys later," I mutter. "I need some air."

As I rise, the chest pains I have been trying to ignore all night grow more intense. They feel like a string of firecrackers exploding inside my chest cavity. The pain grows unbearable. Breathing becomes labored. I loosen my neck tie. Sweat seeps through my pores.

"Someone call an ambulance," I croak, just before slumping forward into a Styrofoam plate loaded with roast beef, green beans, and mashed potatoes with brown gravy.

THE DREAM

"PUSSIES!" is scribbled on the blackboard three times in upper-case letters. Ray Moon sits beside me, a third of his head blown away. His brains are in my lap. A shattered helmet rests between us. Doc Jenkins wraps Ray's head with gauze with the same nonchalance as if he were taping an ankle. Tony Reavis' boots occupy the next seat. Kenny Cain sits on the end of the bench clutching a tumor on his abdomen the size of a football. The rest of the locker room is full of guys who are burned and bleeding and missing limbs. The big colored kid from the Central game is laid out on a stretcher. Linemen sit on the front row, backs on the second row, reserves in the rear. Nobody knows the score. Coach stomps in, mad as a red-assed bee, and starts chewing us out and telling us what a bunch of losers we are. Pretty soon the foaming starts and then he starts drooling and spitting and then he morphs into General Westmoreland – the short gray hair, the dark eyebrows – and he's slobbering about how we

need to go out there and finish what we started. Then he turns into my dad. He looks right at me and says 'You're not hurt, are you son?'"

R ECOVERY

I wake up in a hospital bed with all kinds of tubes and electrodes taped to my limbs and needles poked under my skin. Hog sits at the foot of the bed. He tosses me a sack of clothes, a Bible, a high school yearbook, and some magazines: *Sports Illustrated, Newsweek, Time.*

"How you feeling, Gator?" he asks.

"Like dog shit. What happened?"

"Heart attack. Big one. You almost didn't make it, partner. We were worried about you."

"Thanks, Hog. I'm glad you're here."

"No problem. I love you, man. You're one of us."

"How long have I been here?"

"A couple of days."

"Did we win?" I say, alluding to the time when I was hospitalized with a concussion fifty years before. Hog laughs.

"You looked like you were having a bad dream just before you woke up. You kept saying, 'I'm not hurt...I'm not hurt."

"Yeah, bad dream. I've been having it a lot lately."

"So, Gator, are you saved?" Hog asks out of the blue. "Am I going to see you in heaven?"

The questions come from left field. They are the last questions I expect or want to hear.

"Yes sir," I sputter, mostly to keep Hog from preaching to me.

Even so, it was the truth. I invited Jesus into my heart when I was a kid. And then I re-invited him in Vietnam. I promised him that if he'd get me out of that God-forsaken hell hole, I would give my life to him. War has a way of turning atheists into believers and believers into atheists. I was sincere as hell when I made the promise, but Jesus and I never hung together much—probably because my psyche is such a mess, hardly acceptable digs for the indwelling Christ. Make no mistake: I'm grateful to be alive, but I'm hardly in the mood for a sermon.

"That's good," Hog says. He spits snuff juice into a plastic cup. "I'm glad to hear that. Did you see Jesus when you were dying?"

"Yeah. He was walking straight toward me with a bucket of barbecued wings."

"Seriously?"

"No."

Comic Relief

I stand in my urologist's inner office, pants down to my ankles, legs spread-eagled, fingertips drumming on the edge of a metal counter top. I squint and clench my teeth. Behind me my urologist snaps his rubber glove. He's going in. The phone rings from down at my ankles. It rings again. And a third time.

"Are you going to get that?" asks my urologist.

I bend over and retrieve my cell phone from my trousers pocket. The name Richard Johnson is on the screen.

"What's up, Hog?"

"Guess what!"

"I give up."

"I found Ricky Ferrell. He's in prison, just like I suspected. I got on the internet and found an inmate search site. I entered his name and found him!"

"That's wonderful, Hog. Can I call you back?"

"Is this not a good time?"

"Not really."

"Later, Gator."

I hang up the phone as the good doctor's gloved hand enters my rectum and squeezes my prostate. My muscles tense, my eyes bug out, and my fingers clutch the edge of the counter top the way they clutched the metal bar on the Ferris wheel back in high school. These are the fifteen seconds I dread most every year.

"Feels fine," says my urologist.

"Speak for yourself, Doc," I whimper.

"Is the Viagra still working for you?"

"I don't know. I've still got the same sample you gave me last year."

In Search of Ricky Ferrell

A stained glass cross dangles from the rear-view mirror, and a light snow falls as Hog, wearing a Saints cap, guides his Ford pickup through miles of snowy forests and frozen cornfields, all dusted with snow like powdered sugar on French toast. Houses we pass are festooned in Christmas lights and often have nativity scenes in their front yards. We are on our way to see Ricky Ferrell, who is serving a six-year drug sentence. The original plan was to ride our motorcycles, but the weather forces us into Hog's truck. Between Hog and me is a stack of magazines and a Bible bookmarked somewhere in Ephesians. Christmas music plays on the CD player: *Come, o come Emmanuel....*

"You know, sometimes I think playing on that '61 team was the worst thing that ever happened to me," Hog says. The comment is the last thing I expect to hear.

"Why is that?"

"Because that was the high point of my life. I've been on a long downhill slide since. I've always felt like I had to be perfect. Whatever I did, whether it was one-on-one basketball or some business deal, I felt like I had to win. Losing seemed like a moral failure. So I drank. I drank when I won, and I drank more when I lost."

"I know the feeling, Hog."

The correctional facility is a pink brick building surrounded by a chain-link fence rimmed with razor wire. Hog pulls into the parking lot and leaves his keys and spare change in a tray in his truck.

"Leave your stuff here if you don't want to leave it at the gate," he says. He's been visiting prisons for a while, and he knows the ropes. We walk to the main entrance and push a buzzer. A voice crackles over the intercom like the old loudspeakers at Parkway: "State your name and your business."

"Richard Johnson and Russell Gates to see Ricky Ferrell."

We wait for a second or two for the buzzer. Once inside, we are instructed to wait in the lobby, a room with cinder block walls, a few chairs, and a table with a cheap fiber optic Christmas tree. In a few minutes, a white-haired man with sky-blue eyes appears in a laminated glass window. Hog slides the reading material into the slot beneath the window and picks up the telephone receiver. Ricky picks up a receiver on his side of the wall. I can't hear Ricky's end of the conversation. Hog starts with the usual pleasantries: "How are you, Ricky? Good to see you," but like the Apostle Paul, he gets down to some serious evangelizing before long: "You read that Bible, Ricky. Start with the book of John..."

They speak about five minutes, and then it's my turn. I have no idea what to say.

"Hello, Ricky. Long time no see."

"It's been a while, Gator."

"Keeping busy?"

He shrugs.

"Busy as I can. Mostly shoot baskets out in the exercise yard and lift weights. I'm in good shape. Not so different from boys' school."

"No pool table here?"

"Nope. No pool table. That's the first thing I want to do when I get out of this place: shoot a game of pool."

"When's that going to be?"

"Another year if I behave myself."

"What are you going to do once you're out?"

"Stay out of trouble and live out the rest of my life. My mom died a few months back, and they wouldn't let me out for her funeral." A tear wells up and slides down his face, following the channel of one of the deep wrinkles on his cheek.

"I'm sorry," I say.

"Gator?"

"Yeah?"

"Sorry I was such a dick to you back in high school."

"Don't worry about it. It's forgotten."

The warden walks in and tells us to wrap things up.

"Hey, Ricky. Listen, you behave yourself. See you on the other side? Shoot some pool, maybe?"

"Later, Gator. Thanks for coming."

The sky outside the prison has turned black, the temperature has dropped, and a heavy snow falls. Hog and I pile into the truck, and he turns the key and waits for the heater to kick in. Elvis sings "Blue Christmas" on the radio.

"Let's go home. What do you say?"

"Amen. Let's go home."

EPILOGUE

I veer off the highway and ride my Harley down a country lane and up a steep hill. The air is crisp and the autumn leaves are ablaze in yellow, orange, and red. The smell of wood smoke is in the air. At the top of the hill, I turn down a narrow lane. An Australian cattle dog runs alongside me until the road ends at a steep promontory overlooking the Ohio River, which twists its way toward the Mississippi the same way it did when I used to gaze out of Mr. Madison's homeroom fifty years before. I park my bike under the carport, next to the stack of wood I've laid in for winter, and walk toward the back deck. On the river, a barge laden with coal rounds the bend, pushed by a tugboat. I grab my binoculars, focus upon the side of the boat, and record its name in a logbook along with the names of all the other tugboats I have seen since I have been here. Why I do this I'm not sure.

My home is a modest cabin with a rear deck for sipping coffee and watching sunrises and a front porch for watching sunsets. I've got everything I need here: a small kitchenette, a living room with a wood stove and a big-screen television, a bathroom, and a bedroom/office. I found the place one day when I was out riding and bought it not long after Mom died with money she left me in her will, along with some money from the sale of our house on the hill. Some of the old furnishings from Mom's house have found their way here – the kitchen table, the dishes and cookware, the living room recliner, several chests of drawers, some end tables, and the couch that converts into a bed. My desk rests on the front porch, where I set up my laptop and write. I don't have Internet. Cell phone reception is spotty.

Outside a hammock is slung between two sassafras trees, not far from the satellite dish. I pick up a cracked and tooth-marked Frisbee and toss it. Martha – that was the dog's name when I adopted her -- chases after it, leaps high into the air, catches it in her teeth, brings it back, and lays it at my feet. I stroke the white spot between her ears and toss the disk again. Sometimes we do this for hours.

About the Author

Randy Pease is a journalist, educator, and musician. Recently retired from the University of Southern Indiana, where he taught writing for fifteen years, he has turned his attention away from teaching and toward his first love: writing. Over the years he has been a sportswriter, general assignment reporter, columnist, editor, arts critic, music publisher, and public relations copywriter. He has recorded three CDs: Call Me Ishmael (1997), Sometimes the Moon (2002), and Prodigal Sunshine (2010). Once There Were Green Fields is his first shot at writing a novel.

CPSIA information can be obtained at www.ICGtesting.com
Printed in the USA
LVOW07s1409011214

416489LV00001B/9/P